THE LAST DANCE

It is 1960 when WPC Bobbie Blandford starts her new job as the only woman at Stony End police station. As she chases down runaway cars and errant teenagers, and attempts to investigate the murder of businessman Lionel Mapping, she is unaware that it will raise questions about a life that she had forgotten, as well as her father's death. What does it all have to do with handsome doctor Leo Stanhope, and just who can Bobbie trust in a male-dominated world?

SPECIAL MESSAGE TO READERS

THE ULVERSCROFT FOUNDATION
(registered UK charity number 264873)
was established in 1972 to provide funds for
research, diagnosis and treatment of eye diseases.
Examples of major projects funded by
the Ulverscroft Foundation are:-

- The Children's Eye Unit at Moorfields Eye Hospital, London
- The Ulverscroft Children's Eye Unit at Great Ormond Street Hospital for Sick Children
- Funding research into eye diseases and treatment at the Department of Ophthalmology, University of Leicester
- The Ulverscroft Vision Research Group, Institute of Child Health
- Twin operating theatres at the Western Ophthalmic Hospital, London
- The Chair of Ophthalmology at the Royal Australian College of Ophthalmologists

You can help further the work of the Foundation
by making a donation or leaving a legacy.
Every contribution is gratefully received. If you
would like to help support the Foundation or
require further information, please contact:

THE ULVERSCROFT FOUNDATION
The Green, Bradgate Road, Anstey
Leicester LE7 7FU, England
Tel: (0116) 236 4325

website: www.foundation.ulverscroft.com

SALLY QUILFORD

◆

THE LAST DANCE

Complete and Unabridged

LINFORD
Leicester

First published in Great Britain in 2014

First Linford Edition
published 2015

A catalogue record for this book is available
from the British Library.

ISBN 978–1–4448–2515–2

Published by
F. A. Thorpe (Publishing)
Anstey, Leicestershire

Set by Words & Graphics Ltd.
Anstey, Leicestershire
Printed and bound in Great Britain by
T. J. International Ltd., Padstow, Cornwall

This book is printed on acid-free paper

1

'Stop! Oh stop, you stupid car!'

I was just coming out of Stony End railway station, laden down with luggage, when I heard the petulant cry. I looked up the hill and saw a car rolling towards me, with the young woman chasing after it. She was tall, lithe and beautiful, with the looks of a movie star. The car was a blue Triumph Herald. Thinking she was chasing after some errant lover, who no doubt resembled a matinee idol, it took me a moment to realise that no one sat behind the wheel. It was a runaway car! The driver's door was wide open, causing a further hazard to the traffic on the other side of the road.

Just at that moment, a group of children with a woman whom I took to be their teacher started crossing the road just outside the train station.

This was my chance to put into practice everything I had learned over the past thirteen weeks. I immediately saw myself as the heroine in the unfolding drama. Dropping my bags, I burst into action, running up towards the car, praying I would catch it in time. It occurred to me that if I could just get into the driver's side, I could stop the car before it hurt any of the children. In those fleeting moments I saw their parents crying tears of gratitude for my self-sacrifice, and my new sergeant, whom I had not yet met, giving me a posthumous medal for bravery. You would think that thought alone would have stopped me, but I ploughed on up the hill regardless, determined to be the heroine of the hour.

I didn't know it then but it was slap-bang in the middle of a market day and Stony End's streets were very busy. On the way up the hill a cattle truck pulled out of a side road and started up towards the runaway car. Whether the truck driver was asleep or not paying attention, I did not know, but it slammed into the open door of the car, tearing it off with a sickening crunch.

'Oh no!' cried the young woman chasing the car. 'You stupid, stupid thing.' I was not sure if she spoke of the car or herself, but her indignation in the face of the carnage was unmistakable. Her voice was cultured and I immediately pegged her as a southerner.

I sped up and managed to get to the middle of the road before the car ran me over. With my heart banging like a drum, I lurched headlong into the vehicle before turning awkwardly so that I could reach the pedals. I was vaguely aware of the Cliff Richard song 'Move It' blaring from the wireless.

Just as I managed to slow the Triumph by slamming on the brakes and yanking the hand brake, a red Sunbeam Alpine sports car flew out of the same side road that the lorry had just exited. The Triumph slammed into it with a resounding crash. I was thrown forward, only narrowly avoiding hitting the windscreen, but I was winded and shaking like Elvis Presley's hips. Suddenly a posthumous medal did not seem such an attractive prospect.

Further down the road, the teacher had managed to get the children to safety. I let out a long sigh of relief for that at least. I was a bit less pleased when the teacher looked at me and scowled, as if she thought I was responsible for the whole thing.

'What on earth did you do that for?' said the driver of the red sports car, getting out. He was very tall, very handsome, and reminded me of Richard Burton. He certainly had that 'angry young man' look about him at that moment in time. 'Look at the state of my car. I ought to call the police.'

'Why on earth did you pull out of a junction without looking?' I asked.

'I'm a doctor on my way to an emergency, and I don't usually expect cars to come racing down this hill.'

'It was all my fault,' said a voice

behind us. It was the young woman, who had finally caught up with us. She was a tall, slender girl of about twenty-six, with dark hair and cherry-red lipstick. At the time I wondered if everyone in Stony End was as beautiful as this pair. Time and experience taught me differently. 'I'm sorry, Dr Stanhope,' said the brunette. 'It's my car, and I accidentally left the handbrake off whilst I nipped into the house to fetch my bag. This brave girl stopped it from hitting those children.'

'Look at the damage to my car, Dr North,' Dr Stanhope said again. He seemed to be calming down and I suppose having a car hit his beautiful sports car was not the best start to his day. 'I still think we ought to call the police to sort this mess out.'

'I am the police,' I said, finally having got my breath back.

'God help us,' said Stanhope, looking me up and down, as if to find me wanting. I had only just scraped by the height requirement for WPCs, so I

5

pushed up on my tiptoes slightly to make myself seem taller.

'Roberta?' said the girl, looking at me quizzically.

'Yes, that's right.'

'I'm Dr Annabel North. Would you believe I'm your new landlady? I'll say one thing for you — you certainly know how to make an entrance!'

'She certainly does,' said Stanhope, giving me a long hard look.

Great, I thought. *The first day in my new posting and I'm already making enemies.*

★   ★   ★

In 1960 there were only 2500 women in the police force, and I was one of them. Beatlemania was still three years away. The sexual revolution was even further away. Though it was the sixties, life was pretty much as it had been in the fifties, with cheerful pop songs and Hollywood glamour in films juxtaposed with the remainder of the austerity left over from the war years. Those who had lived through rationing were instilled with a severe disapproval of wastage, and yet the 21st-century generation, who throw millions of mobile phones and plastic milk cartons into landfill, tend to blame us for the polar ice caps melting. That being said, things were cheering up in Britain. Girls wore bright full-circle skirts, and the young men dressed in faux Edwardian style, earning the nickname 'teddy boys'.

Parts of Britain had still not been rebuilt, some fifteen years after the war had ended. Things were improving slowly, for the country and for girls like me who wanted a bit more than to spend their lives in a typing pool or a shop until they married and settled into premature middle age. I saw it too often with my friends. One minute they would be a bobby-soxer, all dressed up to go dancing in the elegant gowns of the time; then marriage would happen and the next week they would be dressed in the same drab frocks as their mothers.

I wanted something a bit more than that. Not that the blue serge uniform I had to wear was the epitome of glamour. Norman Hartnell's air hostess-style uniform for women police officers was some years down the line. But the uniform had been smartened up somewhat from the sack-like garments my valiant predecessors in the Women's Auxiliary Service used to wear. When I wore it, I felt a part of something unique.

It's hard to explain the Women's Service to young women of the 21st century. They expect, quite rightly, to be equal to men, with the same pay and the same career prospects. They probably imagine that we were held back quite a lot. To them the 1950s and early 60s seem like the Dark Ages for women. The fact is that women could very often create their own roles within the police force, and they had a valuable job to do when it came to vulnerable women and children. I was a long way from finding my place in those early days.

Stony End was my first posting as a WPC and I feared it would be my last if things kept going wrong. The incident with Dr North's and Dr Stanhope's cars took place a couple of days before I started at the station. And as for finding my place in the police force — well! The morning I began work, I'd have settled for finding a decent pair of stockings.

'Oh no! Not today, of all days.' I looked down at my finger, which was poking through the fine mesh of my only pair. I had to be at the station by a quarter to six and the shops did not open until nine.

Luckily the ladder was above the knee and also the line of my skirt. I reasoned that even the most vigilant sergeant would not check that thoroughly. I grabbed a bottle of pale pink nail varnish and used it to bind the bottom of the ladder and prevent it running any further. It was a trick my mum had taught me. Brought up in a time of waste not want not, I still do it.

I can't tell you how happy I was when tights were invented. There's not much dignity in bringing down a pickpocket when your stocking tops are showing.

I quickly finished dressing and put together my kit, fitting it all into the voluminous pockets of my uniform. I had a whistle, a tape measure, a torch and a first-aid kit. Unlike the men, I was not allowed a truncheon. It was expected that if there was any real trouble, we helpless little women would call on a male officer to help us.

I went back to the dressing table and sat down, looking at the picture of the handsome man that had pride of place next to my dog-eared copies of *Stone's Justices' Manual* and *Moriarty's Police Law*. They had belonged to my dad and were a bit out of date when I used them, but not much had changed since the war.

'Big day today, Dad,' I said to the photograph. 'I hope you'll be proud of me.' My father, Robert Blandford, stared out at me. I wondered what he would say if he could speak. Though the picture was in black and white, his eyes, which had been blue, were startling. I had inherited Mum's hair — which is euphemistically called strawberry blonde nowadays, but then was definitely called ginger, as well as her green eyes and freckles. My elder brother, Tom, was the image of Dad.

In the picture Dad was dressed in his police uniform, holding his helmet at his side, his sergeant's epaulettes gleaming from some reflected light. 'Mum's not very happy about it,' I said aloud. 'First Tom going to Scotland Yard, and now me in Stony End. But it's what we have to do, Dad. Perhaps you could talk to her. Oh, I don't know how you'd do it. Appear to her in a dream or something. I know she worries, after what happened to you, but there was a war on then. Things are

11

different now. I can't imagine me getting into much trouble here in Stony End, can you?' Dad just gazed back at me. Sometimes I felt sure he understood what I said to him, but on that morning, when I needed him the most, he seemed the furthest away. 'Can't you just give me some inkling that you approve of me joining the police force?'

I was disturbed from my reverie by a gentle tap on the door. Quickly throwing the blanket across the bed and bundling up my clothes, I opened the door.

'Telephone for you, Bobbie,' said Annabel. After being approached by the local constabulary, Annabel had agreed to put me up in her cottage. According to her it was 400 years old. Saving her car had very quickly broken the ice between us, which was more than could be said for my relationship with the Stanhope man, who I learned was called Leo.

'Oh he's just naturally unfriendly,' Annabel had told me over dinner the night before. 'Not in any rude way, normally, but he doesn't mix with us. He does his work at the hospital and in the community, then goes home to that big old house of his. He lives up at Stanhope Manor. If you ask me it needs a woman's touch.' She denied any possibility of being that woman. 'Oh no, he's far too stuffy.'

'This from a woman who talks like the Queen?' I had teased.

'Oh don't tell my mother that. She wants me to marry Prince Charles.'

'He's only eleven years old!'

'That's what I said.'

'Anyway, he'd never marry a commoner. No offence.'

'I'm not a commoner. Daddy is a duke.'

'Oh. So what do I call you? Lady Annabel?'

'Good grief, no. I've done with all that. Annabel will do.'

I went downstairs to the telephone in the hallway. Music was coming from the house next door. It was a new song that I had not heard till the day before, though I've heard it hundreds of times since and can sing every word, albeit out of tune. 'Save the Last Dance for Me' by the Drifters. It had been played so many times since my arrival, I could probably have sung it all the way through then. I picked up the phone tentatively. 'Hello?'

'Hello, Bobbie. It's me.' My mum's voice sounded a long way away, even though she was only just across the Peak District.

'Hello, Mum,' I said warily.

'I know we didn't part well, duck. I don't have to tell you how I feel about you joining the police force.'

'Mum . . . '

'Yes, I know, we've argued about it enough. But I couldn't let you go in on your first day without wishing you well.'

'Thanks, Mum. I'm sorry for all the things I said.' We had parted with some very angry words, many of which I regretted then, as I do now. If we thought about the time in the future when those we love are no longer with us, we would be more careful about what we say in anger. But at the time, Mum had been around for all of my life and I expected her to be around for eternity. 'I do love you, you know.'

'I know, sweetheart, and I love you too. I just wish . . . never mind. We have to make the best of a bad job now.'

I sighed, expecting the same old argument. 'It's not a bad job.'

'We'll see,' said my mum.

I put the phone down and walked back upstairs, lost in thought. I looked at the picture of my father on the dressing table, thinking about the call from Mum. No, it couldn't have been his influence, could it? I shook the thought from my head. It was just a coincidence.

I put my cap on, taking one last look in the wardrobe mirror. 'Once more unto the breach . . . ' I whispered. Only it was not once more. It was the first time unto the breach. I remembered Mum's warnings about the police force.

My mum, Dina Blandford, had been a policewoman until her marriage. According to the rules at the time, marrying meant she had to resign. Things changed during the war, but it was too late for Mum to return; and after dad died, she wanted nothing to do with the force. When first my brother, Tom, joined, and then me, Mum did not take it well, making life at home rather strained.

I took a last look around the comfortable bedroom before leaving for work. It was small but it was mine alone. For most of my life I had shared a bedroom with Mum, letting Tom have the only other bedroom in our bungalow. ('Men need more space,' Mum had insisted). When Tom left home to go down to Scotland Yard, I broached the idea of taking over his bedroom; but Mum had resisted it, just as she had resisted the idea of me leaving home, first for thirteen weeks of police training and then for a posting in Stony End. For some reason the latter had upset

Mum more than anything.

I put it down to her old-fashioned standards. Tom leaving was fine even if he was going to work in the police force. That was what men did. But in Mum's world, young ladies only left home to marry. They did not leave home to go and throw themselves into ju-jitsu training and the possibility of having to deal with thieves and vagabonds. Whatever wanderlust had led my mother into the police force had been cured by her getting married. Or perhaps it was cured by dad getting shot.

'I'm going to be all right, Dad,' I said to his picture. Whether I was saying it for his sake or for mine, I did not know.

Ten minutes later I was at the door of Stony End police station. It was really a couple of houses knocked together. I did not know it at the time, but half the building was the sarge's quarters where, as a widower, he lived alone. The other half was the police station.

An old man, rather the worse for

wear, was coming out. 'Thanks for the warm bed for the night, lads,' he was saying as he ambled out into the early-morning sunlight. Despite the sun, there was still some ice on the roads. Winter had not quite gone, and spring had not quite begun. It could have been a metaphor for my new life as a probationer in the police force.

'Anytime, Reg,' said a voice from inside.

'Well I never,' said the man called Reg. 'It's another woman in a police uniform.'

'Good morning, sir,' I said.

'Is it? I'm not so sure of that. How long will you last?'

'Excuse me, sir?'

'The last time they sent a woman here she lasted a week before asking for a transfer. Mind you, Alf in there told me she made a lousy cup of tea. How are you at making tea?'

'I'm not bad,' I said. 'But I'm not here to make tea. I'm here to be a police officer.'

Reg looked squarely at me and then burst out laughing. 'Yeah, good one. Good one. We'll see.' He wandered down the street, still laughing about the very thought of female police officers. It was something we had to deal with a lot back then.

I watched him, feeling as if I had been put on the back foot. To give myself time to rally my inner resources, I looked around at Stony End. I had seen little of it since I arrived, too shy to go far from the cottage in plain clothes. That feeling took a long time to leave me. My uniform was almost a mask I could hide behind, giving me the courage to go out into the community.

It was a small market town with one pub, the Cunning Woman, which had an off-licence-cum-sweet shop attached; and one church, St Jude's. I seemed to remember he was the patron saint of lost causes, which did not bode well.

There were only about half a dozen large streets in the centre of town, all set around the main square, with alleyways leading off them. The rest of the town spread out like a spider's web into the Peaks, with tiny hamlets and single dwellings dotting the landscape. The square had a mixture of small shops (butchers, bakers and candlestick-makers), a new-style supermarket, a greasy spoon-style café, and higgledy-piggledy cottages. All were built with solid Derbyshire stone, and at that time it was rare to see a brick building. The homes were inhabited by workmen and artisans. I found out that at least one of the cottages housed a family with thirteen children. Now, over fifty years later, only outsiders can afford to buy the cottages and most of them only visit at weekends, making it seem like a ghost town. In 1960 Stony End was a vibrant living, breathing community.

A couple of the cottages, then as now, doubled as tea rooms. Signs in the windows said they only operated during the summer season, when walkers and tourists visited the Peak District.

Another house doubled as a fish and chip shop. That opened every evening at seven, till the pubs closed, but was open from lunchtime on Friday, when it was the custom in those days for everyone to have a fish supper. There was also a transport café-cum-petrol station just a bit further out of town, covering the needs of the lorry drivers that used the town as a cut through to Stockport.

Hoardings advertised Ovaltine and Horlicks. I had been an 'Ovaltiney' as a child and still had my badge and membership card somewhere in my mother's house. When I'd had a few too many Babychams, I could also sing the theme tune.

In those days, long before huge multiplexes, even the smallest towns had a cinema. Stony End's Odeon, set between the post office and the slipper baths, was showing *Ben Hur*. I had seen it six times already, alternating between falling in love with Charlton Heston and Stephen Boyd, depending on my mood at the time. I made a mental note to watch it again, in order to make up my mind once and for all.

A river ran through Stony End, and some of the houses were backed right up to it. Each house had a tiny jetty next to the water, on which stood old garden furniture. I thought that I would love to live in one of those houses, and sit out on the jetty in summer evenings, watching the water ripple gently by. Out of nowhere I heard Mum's voice say, 'Careful, Bobbie, you'll fall in.' I laughed at myself. Even with the miles between us, I was letting Mum's overprotectiveness affect me. Without her to hold me back, I felt I ought to flourish in this place. But old habits die hard, and I still wanted to please her.

Over the bridge and a few hundred yards out of town, on the Stockport road, was an estate of Unity houses that had been thrown up after the war to house those bombed out of the cities. They were only meant to be temporary, yet some are still standing more than fifty years later. Further out of town were various farmsteads, and up on a hill overlooking the whole town was Stanhope Manor. Apparently Dr Stanhope lived there alone with whatever dark thoughts filled his mind. I did not know at the time, but his memories were very dark indeed.

On the opposite hill was Mapping's Ale. Before that were a few allotments, including one with a rather ramshackle green caravan amongst the vegetable plots. There was smoke coming out of a flue on top of the caravan, suggesting it was inhabited.

I had a strange feeling of déjà vu. As far as I knew, I had never been to Stony End. Still, there were many towns in Derbyshire of a similar makeup. If not a brewery, they had some factory. If not Stanhope Manor, there was some big house that everyone looked at with a mixture of longing and envy.

'WPC Blandford, I presume. Were you thinking of coming into the station today? Or are you just planning to decorate Stony End with your presence?'

I turned around to see a middle-aged man glaring down at me. He wore the uniform of a sergeant and was handsome for a man of his age, which must have been at least fifty. I was only twenty-one at the time, so anyone over forty seemed ancient. I immediately saluted.

'Don't salute me. I'm a sergeant. I work for a living. You only salute the inspector and the superintendent, and then only the first time you see them in the day or if you see them out on the streets. Not that either of them dirty their hands, or feet, with beat work.'

'I'm sorry, sir. I was just . . . well I don't know Stony End very well and I wanted to get my bearings.'

'Best do that from in here with us. Don't you think?'

I nodded and followed him into the police station. There was a counter in the waiting room, behind which stood a young policeman with a spotty face.

Several doors led off to various parts of the station, which I soon learned was labyrinthine.

The inside of the station had not changed much since the war years. In fact there were still posters on the walls warning that 'Loose Lips Sink Ships'. Some warned of theft. Another showed Tufty, the squirrel who helped to teach children to cross the road. Behind the desk, on the back wall, were pictures of people wanted in connection with various crimes and a list of missing children.

'In my office,' said the sergeant, opening the door.

I went in, aware that all eyes were on me. 'I didn't mean to be late, sir,' I stammered. I did not want to admit that Reg's words had unnerved me. 'I just . . . well as I said, I don't know Stony End.'

The strange look he gave me would make more sense in the future. 'You will by the end of the week. I'm Sergeant Simmonds.'

'Jack Simmonds?' I knew that name! It was one I had grown up hearing.

'You may call me Sergeant Simmonds, or Sarge,' he snapped back.

'Of course, sir. I'm sorry. It's just that my father had a friend called Jack Simmonds.'

'Let's get one thing clear, WPC Blandford. Your father's friendship is something I will always treasure, but that doesn't get you any breaks in my station. Do you understand?'

'Of course.' My face became hot. I was not the sort of person to ask for favours and I hated that he should think it of me. 'Sir, I didn't . . . ' I wished he would ask me to sit down, but he seemed to be enjoying my discomfort.

'Stop calling me sir. It makes me sound like a headmaster. Around here people call me Sarge. As I was saying, you get no special favours, either for being Robert's daughter or for being a woman. What it means is that you have to work twice as hard to prove yourself.

As you know, you have two years' probation, after which time you'll become a full police officer. If in that time you fail in your duties, you're out. You'll mainly be here to help us deal with women and children.'

'I'm willing to work, sir.'

'Good. Now you can start by making me and the rest of the station a cup of tea.'

'But . . . '

'No buts, Blandford. Make the tea, and if you're lucky I might find you some filing to do.'

I wanted to argue at the injustice of it all, but I guessed I was being tested and was determined to prove my mettle. 'You'd best show me where the kitchen is then, Sarge.'

'I could have got a job in a café,' I muttered to myself as I washed up half a dozen grimy mugs in the small kitchenette. They were the first of hundreds I would wash over the next few years. 'At least I might get free cake.'

27

'What's that?' said a voice from one of the tables in the staffroom. There was an open hatch between the kitchenette and the staff room, but I had not heard anyone come in. It was the spotty-faced lad who had been on the desk. I remembered being told his name was Peter something or other, but the names of my new colleagues had been a bit of a blur, lost in the flurry of nerves that accompanied my quick tour of the station.

'Nothing.'

'Great. I'll have two sugars in mine, please.'

'Do you want arsenic with that?' I murmured, thinking he could not hear me.

'I heard that. Look here, WPC Blandford — just because your dad and the sarge were friends, doesn't mean we're going to go easy on you.'

'Yes, he's already told me that,' I said.

'Yeah, I bet. But we reckon he's trying to replace us all with his own people. Well it won't work, darlin'.'

'I'm not your darlin' or darling, for that matter.' It was rare for me to take an instant dislike to someone, even if I accidentally crashed into their car, but I did not like Peter Porter from the start.

'Constable Porter!' the sarge's voice rung out from the staff room. 'Out here now.'

Porter stood up, the rest of his face reddening to match the pimples.

The sarge came to the hatch. 'You too, Blandford. There's been an incident. The Mapping's Ale dray has dropped its load at Four Lane Ends. Blandford, you direct traffic. Porter, you help to clear the barrels off the road.'

When we reached the Four Lane Ends — which I learned was a crossroads on the edge of the town — it was to find chaos and broken barrels.

In those days it was not unusual to see horse-drawn carriages on the roads. There weren't as many automobiles as we're used to seeing today. In the early sixties some milkmen still used drays, as did a few breweries.

I'd had some training in directing traffic at the training school in Warrington, but with my nerves on edge, I forgot everything I had learned. Soon traffic was backed up on all four roads leading to the crossroads.

The drayman, who was called Harris, and Constable Porter were doing their best to clear up the barrels, but one had split and was spewing ale all over the road. A couple of men from the town, including the one called Reg, had come along with various jugs and water carriers to save what they could. There was almost a party atmosphere. With my mouth getting drier, I could have done with a pint myself, but drinking on duty was forbidden then as it is now.

As I tried to move the traffic around the debris, I heard soft laughter. Turning, I noticed for the first time that Leo Stanhope was behind me, sitting in his sports car. It had already been repaired. Or maybe, with all his money, he had more than one. He leaned his head out of the side of the car and smiled at me and for the first time I was able to take in his features properly. He was around thirty years of age, and incredibly handsome, with thick dark curls and strong-looking shoulders. Only now I was closer and not so angry did I notice a fine scar down his cheek. If anything it added to his attraction, giving him a slightly dangerous air.

'Congratulations,' he said, with a wry smile that was far more charming than it should have been under the circumstances. 'You seem to have managed to stop the traffic in Stony End yet again.'

My first instinct was to arrest him for being so darn handsome. There must be something about it in *Moriarty's Police Law*. With my pique and embarrassment of our previous meeting gone, I grinned back at him and said, 'They said I'd never amount to anything.'

'So what's caused all this?'

'The dray from Mapping's Ale.'

'That's Lionel Mapping for you.

Most civilised people would use a lorry, but Mapping still believes in working people and horses to death.' There was some bitterness in his voice and I guessed there was something personal behind the remark.

As he spoke, a message came over the police car radio. I went to the black Zephyr, which they had parked on the verge, and answered. It was Simmonds. 'What is it, Sarge?'

'Where's Porter?'

'He's still helping to lift the barrels, Sarge.'

'I need him to go up to Mapping's Ales. Mr Mapping has been found dead. Tell Porter I'm sending a detective along in another car to pick him up.'

'I could go, Sarge.'

'You stay where you are, directing traffic until the road is clear. And remember to charge the dray driver with obstructing the highway.'

'Porter!' I called, seething. I wanted to be in the thick of things, even though

I'd been warned, not just by the sarge but by all my instructors in the training camp, that women just didn't get to do that in the police. I guess I wanted to run before I could walk, and that was even harder for a woman.

'What?' Porter walked across to me, carrying his jacket, which he had taken off in order to help move the barrels.

'You have to go up to Mapping's Ales. It seems Mr Mapping has been found dead.'

I forgot how close Dr Stanhope was until I heard him make a strangled sound. He suddenly did a U-turn and screeched off back along the Stockport road, leaving black tyre tracks in his wake.

2

'Odd to see him out,' said Porter, watching Leo Stanhope drive away. 'He usually just locks himself away up at Stanhope Manor unless he's in his surgery or dealing with patients. Wonder what got his goat.'

'Me too,' I said, but I did not really want to discuss it with Porter. I tried to put Leo Stanhope out of my mind. 'I could go with you up to the brewery. It would be good for me to learn about murders and the like.'

'First of all, we don't know it's murder yet and secondly, you have traffic to direct. Sarge's orders. I heard him, you know.'

'You're supposed to be helping to move the barrels. It's odd how you can be taken off a job, but I can't.'

'I'm senior to you.'

'No you're not. You're the same rank,

and I've heard you're still on probation.' Porter still had eighteen months to go.

'But I'm a man, which makes me senior.'

'No it doesn't.'

'I haven't got time to argue.' Porter grinned maliciously. 'The sarge has given me important work to do.' He winked and clicked his tongue. 'Never mind, gorgeous. At least you can keep all the drivers happy. If they get too angry, just show them your stockings, though I'd hide that ladder if I were you.'

I imagined slapping his silly face, at the thought of him looking up my skirt, but thought better of it. My first day was going badly enough. The detective sergeant, who I later found out was called Marshall, arrived in a black police car, swerving around the standing traffic and going off-road slightly to get around what was left of the barrels. Porter jumped into the car and waved to me, smirking as he went.

Without another officer there to judge me, I managed to sort out the traffic much better. Soon the dray was loaded again and Harris the driver was up on the cart, ready to go. 'Thanks, miss,' he said. 'I was hoping to get home early today, because the wife is about to have the baby, but it's not going to happen now.'

'Did you see Mr Mapping this morning?' I asked, curious about the dead man.

'Yeah, as I was loading up the cart. Is it right he's dead?'

'We can't confirm that right now,' I said, trying to sound officious.

'There's nowt kept secret around here, miss. I heard PC Porter talking about it. Mapping was his usual grumpy self when I saw him, but we're all used to that with him. Mind you, they reckon he had some charm in his younger days, but he wasn't a man's man. Didn't talk about the football or anything like that. Fancied himself with the ladies though, by all accounts.'

'So he's not a nice man then?'

Harris shrugged. He did not seem very upset to hear of his employer's death. 'They say he made his money on the black market during the war, and since then he has pretty much taken over Stony End.'

'Not anymore,' I said.

'I suppose not,' Harris said. 'Though I don't know what'll happen about Mapping's Gold.'

'Mapping's Gold?'

'The new ale they're rolling out in a few months. Was going to save the company from ruin, it was.'

'So he had money worries?'

'Not in the way you or I do. You know what these rich folks are like. If they have to go a year without buying a new car, they think they're living in poverty. They should try living in two rooms with a load of kids on the wages they pay us. Who knows, maybe Dr Stanhope will step up now and do what needs to be done for Stony End.'

I wondered at that, and why it was up

to Leo Stanhope to take care of Stony End. Two world wars were supposed to have ended the days of the local laird overseeing the local populace, but in Derbyshire things moved a bit more slowly, and those from the lower classes often still looked to the middle and upper classes for guidance. The culture of deference had not quite died. 'And you're sure Mapping was okay when you left him?'

'Yep. Now I come to think of it, Mr Mapping wasn't too mardy today. He was whistling when I first saw him. That probably means he'd done someone out of something.'

'How did you manage to lose the barrels? I'll have to give you a ticket, I'm afraid.' I probably should not have been that apologetic, but Harris seemed like a nice bloke.

'I don't know. I usually put them on securely enough. But I was just coming down here, past old Mrs Higgins, and suddenly they all come adrift.'

'Were you in a hurry?'

'If you mean did I kill Mr Mapping then use the dray as a getaway car . . . no miss, I didn't.'

Even I had to smile at the incongruity of that. 'I suppose not. So did Mr Mapping have many enemies?'

'The man was all about enemies, miss. Only his daughter and his secretary seemed to love him. Now if you'll excuse me, I must get on or I'll never get home to my Florrie.'

I had no choice but to let him go, even though I would have liked to question him further. His dray was still blocking part of the road and the sooner he moved, the sooner I could go about my own business.

Porter, as annoying as he was, had a point. No one had said that Mapping had been murdered. But what if Harris had killed him, then acted as if nothing had happened? Or what if his killer was amongst those caught up in the traffic jam?

Leo Stanhope had been coming from the other direction, so it could not have been him. Unless he had killed Mapping then come back to the town by a roundabout route. Lots of roads led in and out of Stony End, with dozens of tiny back lanes set amongst the Peaks.

As I turned ready to return to the station, I almost bumped into a woman dressed in a tweed suit and sensible brogues. Her dark hair was pinned back in a bun. I put her age at about forty, but it was hard to tell as she seemed to be one of those women who had become old before her time. 'Sorry, madam,' I said.

'That's all right, WPC,' she said in cool tones. 'What's going on here?'

I was already aware that news of Mr Mapping's demise had got out to both Dr Stanhope and Mr Harris, and I did not want to be responsible for breaking the news to someone who might be a relative before the man's death had been confirmed. 'Just the dray dropped its load, madam. All is clear now. Are you going to Mapping's Ales?'

'Yes, I'm Mr Mapping's secretary, Mrs Garland.'

'Ah . . . ' I wondered whether to ask her about him, but already feared I'd said too much. 'We're neighbours. I'm lodging with Dr North.'

'Really?' Her disinterest disappointed me and I realised then we were never going to be good friends. 'I must be going,' she said. 'I'll be late for work and Mr Mapping will not stand for it.'

I resisted the urge to say that Mr Mapping would not be standing for anything anymore, but I had decided I would be more professional, after blurting everything out to Mr Harris.

Mrs Garland carried on walking up the road towards the brewery. I wondered whether I should stop her. Deciding that the detective sergeant might want a word with her, I let her go, thinking that despite her prim appearance and prematurely aged face she had good legs. I was only a little bit pleased to see that one of her stockings had a ladder in the back. It proved that it could happen to the best of us.

'You there, missy — what's your name?'

I spun around to see an elderly woman standing at the side of the caravan I had noticed earlier. She was very strange-looking, the antithesis of the elegant Mrs Garland. The old woman wore mismatched clothes, including a brown A-line skirt and a purple sweater, over which she wore a man's military great coat, despite it being quite a warm day. On her head was a black beret. I had never seen anyone quite like her before, and I've never seen anyone like her since. I did not know it then, but the people I was meeting in those early days were to form an important part of my life in Stony End. At the time, she just seemed like a strange old woman with very bad dress sense.

'WPC Blandford, Mrs . . . erm?'

'Blandford, hey? Now where have I heard that name before? It'll come to me, I'm sure. I'm Mrs Higgins. Martha

Higgins. Come here. I have a complaint to make.'

'What is it, Mrs Higgins?'

Mrs Higgins came to the gate at the bottom of her garden and opened it. 'Someone has trampled on my cabbages.'

'Oh . . . well, it was probably children.'

'The feet are a bit too big for children. Not that the little blighters don't cause havoc. Come and have a look. I've seen the films and television. You can take moulds or something now, can't you?'

'I'm not sure the sarge — I mean Sergeant Simmonds would allow moulds to be used just to stop someone trampling cabbages. Unless something was stolen . . .'

'I like the way you think, my girl.' I opened my mouth to protest that I had not been thinking of stolen cabbages, on account of secretly considering such a petty crime was beneath my abilities. Still, it was my first day and I was eager to impress the locals with my detective abilities. I could not imagine Porter taking the time to worry about cabbages, so in a sudden change of mindset I decided to catch the cabbage patch crumpler if it was the last thing I did. 'Come on in, and tell me all about yourself.'

'Very well. I'll come and take a look.'

'Good girl. Come on in.'

I did not much like the idea of going into the caravan, but I was too afraid of Mrs Higgins to refuse. The caravan looked very grubby from the outside and I realised that what I had taken to be green paint from a distance was in fact moss. Inside turned out to be a revelation. Though undoubtedly old and in need of repair, Mrs Higgins kept the caravan spotlessly clean, with comfortable cushions and rugs giving it a homely feel.

'Lovely,' I said, sitting down on one side of the dinette. On the far end of the table was a television set. Mrs Higgins must be better off than she looked, or she had got the television from Radio Rentals. These were the days before every home had a television in every room.

Even one was a rarity. I had seen television at a friend's house, when the Queen was crowned, but Mum had always resisted getting one, insisting it would lead to the loss of morals in the nation. I must admit it made television seem like a guilty pleasure; but whenever I had seen it, at a friend's or in a shop window, the only programmes on were *Pinky and Perky* or an American programme called *I Love Lucy*, and I was not quite sure how they were contributing to the decline of society as we knew it.

'I like it here,' I said.

Mrs Higgins smiled at my compliment. 'Much better than living in a dusty old house.'

'Have you ever lived in a house?' I asked her. 'Or are you a gypsy?'

'I did travel with the gypsies once,

not long after my stint in the French resistance.' As she spoke, Mrs Higgins lifted a kettle from an ancient coal-fired stove that took up a good bit of the caravan.

'You speak French?'

'Not a word,' said Mrs Higgins. 'But it's all hand gestures over there anyway, isn't it?'

'I really don't know,' I said warily. 'It must have been a very exciting time.'

'Oh yes. Not as exciting as bull-fighting with Hemingway, but fairly exciting. He still sends me postcards — from Cuba mainly.'

'Oh.'

Mrs Higgins put a fine china cup in front of me. 'No saucer, I'm afraid. I like to save on washing up. I did enough of that for old King George at Buckingham Palace.'

'George the Third?' I suggested.

'Tsk. No, silly. The Fifth. Not that madness doesn't run in the family. They keep it very quiet.'

'I'll bet.' My head was spinning as I

wondered just how reliable Mrs Higgins was. Of course it was possible that she had been in the French resistance, served the royal family and gone out drinking with Hemingway, but it did not seem likely. 'Now, about your cabbages. Did you say one was stolen?'

'If it gets your people out here with a mould, then yes. One was stolen. I'm sure I had six left and now there's only five. Will that do?'

'I should think so. When do you think it was taken?'

'It must have been this morning. There were no footprints last night.' Mrs Higgins sat opposite me, with her own cup of tea cradled in her hands. She wore fingerless gloves, and I was to learn that she kept them on in all weathers, even when the sun was high in the sky.

'Did you see anyone?'

'No, I was in the bath when it happened.'

I remember looking around the

caravan, wondering where that could possibly be!

'In a small outhouse, around the back,' said Mrs Higgins, as if reading my mind. 'I have a bath a week, whether I need it or not.' She laughed at her own joke. 'I heard something, but by the time I came out it was all over, and the dray had shed its load. So, now you tell me. What's happened with Mr Mapping?'

'I wish I could tell you,' I said. Mrs Higgins's caravan was so homely and she so approachable that I forgot all about being professional. 'They say he's been found dead, but I'm not allowed to be part of that investigation. This is a lovely cup of tea by the way.'

'Get it from the Windsors every Christmas. Edward and Mrs Simpson to you. I was always on their side.'

'I see.'

'I must say it's rare to see a policewoman around these parts. I used to work at Scotland Yard, but I had to work harder than the men.'

'My brother is at Scotland Yard,' I told her. 'Tom Blandford.'

'Don't know him. Probably after my time.'

'He's a proper detective, plain clothes and everything. I'd love to be a detective, but I bet it won't happen.'

'Don't let those men put you down, Miss Blandford. We women have to fight harder, but we get there in the end.'

'I hope so. Has Stony End never had a policewoman stay for a long time? Not even during the war?'

'I wasn't here then, but I don't think so. It's all old boys together. You know the type. Funny handshakes and baring a nipple.'

'Of course, you were off fighting in the Resistance in the war,' I mused.

'You don't believe a word I say, do you?'

'Well . . . '

Mrs Higgins laughed. 'I've done a bit of fortune-telling in my time. Have you finished your tea?'

'Yes, thank you.'

Mrs Higgins took my cup and then reached up to the cupboard above the dinette, from where she took a saucer. 'I'll not worry about the washing-up for once,' she said, flipping the cup over and then turning it three times. She flipped it back over and looked at the tea leaves.

'Ah, I see a man in your life.'

'Really?' In those days it was all right to admit you'd quite like to be married and have children, even if you did have your own career. Like all girls, I dreamed of 'the one', but thus far my efforts to find him had failed. I'd thought I had found 'the one', but he turned out to be someone else's.

'According to this you already have met him. In a . . . let me see . . . yes, a red sports car. Scarred but very handsome. A man who hides from the world. You might just be *his* saviour.'

'I really ought to go,' I said, feeling unnerved. 'I'll ask at the station about taking moulds from your cabbage patch.'

I was back at the station when I realised that Mrs Higgins had seen more of what happened at the cross-roads than she let on, including me talking to Dr Stanhope. The old woman was just teasing me and I fell for it!

'Sarge,' I said, when I saw Sergeant Simmonds in the waiting room. 'I wonder if I could take a mould. Mrs Higgins said someone stole her cabbages. I thought I could get the perpetrator's footprints.'

'I don't think so,' said Simmonds. 'We've got a possible murder on our hands. Mrs Higgins's cabbages can go and . . . ' He took a deep breath as if checking himself. 'Forget Mrs Higgins's cabbages, that's what I'm saying. I need you to go and sell some raffle tickets for the policemen's ball.'

'So Mr Mapping was murdered then,' I said, perhaps a little too eagerly. After all, it was a man's life we were talking about. On the other hand I did not know him, so his death meant nothing to me. 'Couldn't I go and help out up there? I'd like to sit in on a real murder mystery. I could go with you to inform the family. I'm told that's part of my duties.'

'No, you can't come. You don't get a big murder case on your first day, Blandford.' It seemed really unfair, and I believed I was not being allowed to do my job properly. Simmonds picked up a book of tickets from the counter. 'Raffle tickets, now! Sixpence each or five for two shillings. Can you ride a bike?'

'Yes, Sarge.'

'Good, because you can't take the car. I need it to go and see Mr Mapping's family. They're important around here and need the personal touch.' Something about the way he said it suggested that he did not necessarily agree with that. 'There's a bike around the back of the station. Use that.'

Trying not to pout, I took the raffle tickets and went through the station house, to where there was a back yard in which all manner of things were stored, including clapped-out old police cars. I looked around for a bicycle, but could not see one.

'In the shed,' said a voice from the back door. I looked back to see Simmonds standing at the door, looking at me in a strange way. I hoped he was not going to be difficult. I had already had a problem with one of my male lecturers at the training centre making a pass at me and threatening to give me bad grades if I did not, as he said it, 'put out'. I got around him by threatening to 'put out' to his wife that he was a lecherous old goat.

Then again Simmonds had shown no such interest in me, and in fact seemed rather irritated by my presence in his station. But there was something there. Perhaps, I thought glumly, it was because he had known my father and found me wanting.

I opened the shed door and exclaimed happily. It was not a

53

bicycle, but a Vespa 125 scooter. 'This? Really?'

'That's the one. It's yours to use, so you might as well take it home with you at nights. None of the lads would be seen dead on it. Some of the locals associate the scooter too much with those mods and rockers that are starting to cause trouble all over, and neither group are popular around here. But you're a girl, so you'll be okay.'

'Oh wonderful!' I said without irony. 'It's just like *Roman Holiday*. Except there's no Gregory Peck to share it with.'

I heard Simmonds tut and slam the back door, but I did not care. The bike was a dream come true and I loved that it was all mine!

A few minutes later I was riding through the streets of Stony End, having forgotten about selling raffle tickets, as the wind rushed through my hair. It was a freedom such as I had never known. Luckily I had thought to take off my cap and secure it on the back of the bike.

I saw more of the town than I had managed so far, including the tiny alleys where back-to-back houses vied for space. I rode out into the country-side where the houses were further apart, then back down into the town past the hospital and the little school opposite the train station, where I could hear children singing.

It all seemed so familiar, and yet I could have sworn that I had never been to Stony End before. I put it down to so many Derbyshire towns looking similar, but that did not rid me of the feeling of déjà vu.

I would have also sworn that I did not intend to visit Stanhope Manor, and yet the Vespa rolled up outside its gates. Clearly the scooter had a mind of its own. The red sports car was in the driveway. 'Raffle tickets,' I mumbled to myself as the front door opened and Leo Stanhope appeared. 'I'm here to sell raffle tickets.'

'I'm here to sell raffle tickets for the

policemen's ball,' I said when I had walked up to the door, leaving the Vespa at the bottom of the long driveway. The manor house was truly magnificent, of Georgian design. But it also looked cold and uninviting.

'There's an answer to that I dare not voice,' Dr Stanhope said, his lips curving into that wicked grin.

As I realised his meaning, I blushed profusely. Regaining my equilibrium, I chose to ignore him. 'We're raising money. It's for charity.'

'If you're the prize, I'll buy the whole book,' he said.

I did not know how to answer that one! A few days earlier he was angry with me for damaging his precious car, and now he spoke of winning me in a raffle. 'I'm not. It's, erm . . . there's a hamper, I think and some bottles of wine.'

'I know. I provided the hamper.'

'You did? That was very kind of you, Dr Stanhope.'

'Would you like to come in? I'll have

to get some cash.'

I hesitated. What if he was some madman? My training had warned me against such things. I knew I ought to have brought a man with me. Irritated by the idea of my own helplessness, I pushed the thought aside and followed him into the house. I may not have a truncheon, but I had learned a form of ju-jitsu. I was ready for any eventuality — well, apart from that of falling in love with him; and to be honest, that did not seem to be much of a problem at the time. Yes he was beautiful to look at, and my heart fluttered a little every time I saw him because of his movie-star looks, but it was not love. At least not then. By the time it was love, the past conspired against us.

'I'll just get some money from the kitchen. Wait there.'

The parts of the manor house I saw that day had the same barely-lived-in effect. The hallway was magnificent, with a large curving staircase that made me think of *Gone with the Wind*. That made me blush again, remembering the scene where Rhett Butler swept Scarlett up in his arms. Only, Leo did not look like Clark Gable. Thank goodness. I never did much like those ears and that funny thin moustache.

'Is there a Mrs Butler ... I mean Stanhope?' I asked him when he returned from the back of the house.

'No. Unless you mean my mother, and she's dead.'

'I'm sorry.'

'No need. Our parents died several years ago.'

'Our? You have brothers and sisters?'

'Just a sister.' His face darkened and I wondered what the story was there. 'I'll take five.'

'Five what?'

'Raffle tickets.'

'Of course. Sorry. Yes. Oh ... ' Despite all my supposed calm, I was behaving like an idiot around him. 'I've left them on the back of the scooter.'

Leo smiled again. 'I'll walk back

58

down with you, shall I? Save you the trip back.'

'Yes, it's probably best. I'm not having a good first day.'

'Everyone's first day at work is a bit awful,' he said as we walked back to the bike.

'Was yours?'

'Pretty much. I nearly dropped a newborn baby. The books don't warn you what slippery little beggars they are.'

'Oh gosh! Was it all right?'

'Yes, and he is now a strapping five-year-old.'

'Are you from a family of doctors?'

'No. We owned the brewery, but Mapping bought my parents out.'

'Mapping? Oh yes — why did you rush off when you heard he was dead?'

'I had to go and tell someone.'

'Who?'

'That's really none of your business.'

'Of course it's my business. A man has been murdered. Possibly. I mean, he may not have been, and no one has said that yet.' I was not doing very well at all, and wished my mouth would just stop moving. 'I'm a police officer.'

'You're a police officer who directs traffic while her male colleague goes to investigate.'

'Well, we seem to be here.' I seethed silently, trying to remain calm and professional. To be undermined by the men in the station was one thing. I had expected it. But to be undermined by a member of the public, and a very handsome member of the public at that, was another matter. I snatched the raffle tickets out of the bag on the back of the scooter and clumsily ripped five off. 'That'll be two shillings please.'

Dr Stanhope handed me the money and took the tickets. 'Thank you, erm . . . Sorry, I don't remember your name.'

That stung a bit, but I let it go. I had not forgotten him. 'WPC Blandford.'

He frowned and I got the feeling he was annoyed with my name, but I did not know why. 'Do you have a first name?'

'Most people do.'

'I'd like to know yours.'

'Why? I'm just a useless policewoman who directs traffic. Good day, Dr Stanhope.' I got onto the scooter and started it up.

'WPC Blandford, I'm sorry for what I said. I've had a really bad day today. A bad night in fact.'

'Let's forget it, shall we?' I gave him a tight smile, but I was still hurt by his jibe about directing traffic. Not to mention his forgetting my first name. I had not forgotten him.

As I set off back towards the town, letting the breeze cool my fevered cheeks, I began to wonder, uncharitably, whether Dr Stanhope's bad day had started with the murder of Mr Mapping. At least that would give me a reason to lock him up so those dark good looks did not torment me anymore.

★   ★   ★

On that first day I stayed later at the station than I should have. After I had sold most of the raffle tickets I was put on filing, and as soon as the men realised I could type with more than two fingers I was expected to type up everyone's notes. It occurred to me I should have stayed as a receptionist. I hoped it would mean that I'd get to see details of the mysterious Mr Mapping's death, but they kept those away from me.

At seven o'clock I finally got onto the Vespa and started out of town. As I passed the chip shop, the tangy smell of vinegar on battered fish made my mouth water and I realised how hungry I was. 'Fish, chips and some fish bits, please,' I said when I got to the counter.

I remember, years later, going into a chip shop in Wales and asking for fish bits and they had looked at me gone out. They were simply the crunchy bits of batter that had come off the fish during the frying process, and in Derbyshire they were, and still are, considered a great delicacy. I still love a few on my chips, even though my teeth don't cope with them too well now that I'm elderly.

'So you're the new WPC,' said the woman behind the counter. She was around the same age as my mother, with peroxide-blonde hair and thick foundation that seemed to be melting under the heat.

'I am.'

'They say your name is Blandford. Bobbie Blandford.'

'That's right.'

'Any relation to Dina and Robert?'

'Dina is my mum. Robert was my dad. How do you know them?'

'Don't you remember me? I was your 'aunty Dot'. No relation, but me and your mum were good friends at school. Dotty and Dina, the Double Ds, they called us. You used to live here when you were a little girl. You lived in a house along the river there. Until your dad got shot, bless his heart. I haven't seen your mum in years. How is she?'

3

By the time I reached home, I had no appetite for my fish and chips. How could I not have known we'd lived in Stony End or that it was where my father had died?

So much of that first day made sense to me now. Why I had recognised Stony End, despite being sure I had never been there. Why some people, including Mrs Higgins and Dr Stanhope, had recognised my name. But Dr Stanhope could not have been more than ten years older than me. It made me wonder what else I did not know. How much had my mother kept from me? And why?

'Oh that smells good,' said Annabel. She was just letting herself into the cottage when I arrived back, and carrying a white sack of what seemed to be flour. 'I wish I'd called for some.'

'You can have these. I'm not hungry now.'

'Why? What's happened, sweetie? No, on second thought, save it for later. I've got some Babycham in the fridge. Bring the fish and chips and we'll share them, then you can tell me all about it.'

We shared the fish and chips and a glass of Babycham in Annabel's sitting room. It would become my sitting room too, but I'd only been there a few days and I still felt a bit like an interloper, so I had stayed in my room, apart from at meal times in the kitchen. But Annabel said it was 'eating by the fire' time. In the future that was to prove to be a regular event for us, due to our irregular shift patterns. We'd sit there for hours talking, or watching television — our favourite shows were *Opportunity Knocks, Dixon of Dock Green* and *Armchair Theatre* — and eating whatever came to hand. Cheese on toast, Spam sandwiches and cake, or if we finished work at the right time fish and chips, with fish bits. They were new to

Annabel, due to her being from London, and I felt glad to be able to introduce her to a bit of Derbyshire.

I crunched on a fish bit that had been drenched in vinegar and felt my appetite return immediately. Having someone to chat to also helped. Annabel, like most doctors, was a good listener.

'This is lovely,' I said, when I first saw how Annabel had decorated the room with modern furnishings. It was more like a London apartment than a country cottage. The only slightly out of place decoration was a skeleton in the corner. 'Meet Georgina,' said Annabel.

'Hello, Georgina.' I shook the skeleton by the hand.

As we ate and drank our Babycham, I told her all about my father. 'I didn't even know we lived in Stony End.'

'What did your mum tell you?' asked Annabel.

'She said that when I was three years old, during the war, my father was killed in the line of duty. That's why I wanted to become a policewoman, to honour him, even though Mum is not happy about it at all. But they never said where it happened, and I suppose I always assumed it must have been in Chesterfield. All I know is that he went out one night, in plain clothes, to stake out a place where there was going to be a robbery. Black marketers, they said. The killer was arrested and sent to jail. I've always accepted it at face value and never really asked questions. Some detective I am!'

'We don't question what our parents tell us,' said Annabel. 'Why should you? If the perpetrator was found and punished, then what else is there to know?'

'This morning I'd have said you were right, but now I'm not so sure. There's a whole part of my life I don't know about. This morning, I had a vision of Mum telling me to be careful on the jetty of a house by the river, except at the time I thought it was just her influence catching up with me. Now I think that it really happened. It makes me wonder what else I don't know.'

'There's only one way to find out. Get out your dad's case files. They're bound to be at the police station somewhere.'

'Yes, if they ever let me near to them! At the moment I'm making tea, typing up everyone's reports and directing traffic! I knew it would be hard to be a woman in the police force, but it's even more frustrating than I imagined! My biggest mystery today was whether to buy Tetley or PG Tips.'

'Try being a woman doctor,' Annabel said, biting into a chip. 'I have a degree in medicine, yet I'm given the jobs that the nurses should do. It's not that I think I'm better than the nurses, but if I'd wanted to become a nurse I would have taken up nursing. That's what my mum did. I want to be a doctor like my dad. Today I spent most of my time in accident and emergency, putting Plaster of Paris onto a broken arm. I know how to do it, but I was so mad because I know that none of the male doctors would do it, that I made a complete hash of it. The men would give the job to a nurse. Oh, that reminds me. I have to practise. I was going to use Georgina, but she's a bit lacking in the flesh department. Can I borrow your arm?'

'Why not?' I grinned. 'Give Georgina the night off. She's looking a bit under the weather.'

Annabel fetched the bag that she had been carrying earlier. It said 'Plaster of Paris' on the side. There was something quite warm and comforting about the strips of bandage dipped in the material. That, and the glass of sparkling perry, made me feel a bit woozy and silly.

'They wouldn't even let me get the footprints from Mrs Higgins's garden,' I moaned, as we traded stories of women being treated badly in the workplace.

'A male doctor told me today that I'll get nowhere unless I sleep with him,'

Annabel complained.

'I haven't had that yet, though Peter Porter is a bit of a pest. The odd thing is, I don't think he even likes me. He just says things that he thinks he's expected to say as one of the lads. But I've been thinking. About Mrs Higgins's garden.'

'The Case of the Crumpled Cabbage,' said Annabel, bursting into giggles.

'Don't you start!' Rather than be angry, I giggled too. 'No, listen. I think it's linked to Mr Mapping's death.'

'Mapping? Oh they brought him into A&E today. He'd drowned in a vat of beer. They thought he'd fallen in, but I found marks on his head.'

'You did? What sort of marks?'

'Like the shape of an M. It had been pressed into his head with something.'

'M for Mapping?'

'Yes, I suppose so. Like a brand.'

'There was an M burnt into the side of the barrels this morning.'

'Really?'

'Yes, so someone might have held him under the beer with a branding iron.'

'What a way to go,' said Annabel. 'Sorry, I shouldn't laugh, but he really was an odious man. He really fancied himself where women were concerned. I gather he was a good-looker in his day, but a man of that age chatting up girls of our age is a bit creepy if you ask me.'

As we chatted, music started up. It was 'Save the Last Dance for Me'. 'Doesn't that person have another record?' I asked. 'Who is it?'

'That's Mrs Garland. She works at Mapping's. She's . . . she was Mr Mapping's secretary.'

'Oh yes, I met her the other day. She was on her way to work.' I had a brilliant idea. 'I could ask her about him.'

'She wouldn't tell you. She's fiercely loyal to him. God knows why. When I first started at the hospital six months ago, Mr Mapping's wife used to come in a lot. Always walking into doors, tripping over things. You know the type.'

I nodded sagely. I'd been warned about domestic violence and how hard it was to get a woman to press charges.

'But one day she came in with Garland,' Annabel continued, 'who had been told to bring her. Mrs Mapping had broken ribs. I tried to gently suggest that she seek help and perhaps leave her husband, at which point Jane Garland became furious and took me aside. Mr Mapping was not capable of such a thing, she said, and it was not his fault he had such a clumsy wife.'

'So could his wife have killed him?'

'Not likely. She died not long after.' Annabel looked sad, and I sensed her feeling of failure over Mrs Mapping.

'Did he kill her, do you think?' I asked.

'You'd think so, wouldn't you? But no, she died of a heart attack. I daresay the stress he caused her did not help. There . . . ' Annabel patted the last bit of plaster into place. 'Your arm should mend in about six weeks.'

'So how do we get it off?'

'Oh I don't know. I think I have to sleep with an orthopaedic surgeon to learn that bit.' Annabel winked. She went to her doctor's bag and took out a scalpel. 'I'll try not to cut your arm off.'

It took some time, but eventually my arm was free again. I bade Annabel good night and then went to bed, sinking down into the mattress. One thing about Annabel is that she knew how to be comfortable and how to make others comfortable. After years of sharing with my mother and then sleeping on army beds at the training camp, a huge double bed with a satin duck-down quilt was more luxury than I had ever known.

But I could not sleep. My head was too full of the day's events. The revelation about my father was uppermost in my mind. I had so many unanswered questions and I knew it was not something I could ask my mother about. Maybe my brother knew more, but he was not there. I was on the scene, as it were, and probably in the best place to learn the truth. I decided there and then that I would not bother the family with it.

My thoughts drifted to Mr Mapping. I hardly knew the man, and whilst any death was sad, by all accounts few would miss him. That in itself was a little bit sad. One always hopes one will be missed. I was nearly asleep when I remembered Mrs Higgins's words about having heard something and that by the time she came out of her makeshift bathroom, the dray had shed its load.

At the time I had laughed at the idea of Mr Harris using the dray as a getaway cart, but I got to thinking: what if someone else had been hidden on the cart, and the barrels come adrift when they jumped off? Amongst the chaos they could easily evade capture, and there was a copse behind Mrs Higgins's plot into which they could have disappeared.

I knew I needed to get those prints and once the idea was in my head, I could not sleep. It might be too late. Mrs Higgins could have tidied the cabbage patch over. I just had to hope that she was expecting me to go back.

When I got up in the morning, it was to find my arm covered in white powder left over from the plaster cast. That was when the solution hit me.

'Of course!' I exclaimed as I washed it off and dressed quickly. I ran to Annabel's room and knocked on the door.

'Plaster of Paris,' I gasped, out of breath. 'I need it for Mrs Higgins's cabbage patch . . . please.'

'Oh that's brilliant, Sherlock! I'm coming with you!'

* * *

Mrs Higgins had not changed anything about the cabbage patch, and a slight frost overnight had ensured that the ground was nice and hard when we arrived with the plaster.

'I'm her Dr Watson,' Annabel explained to Mrs Higgins. 'Except my name is Dr North. Annabel North.'

'A woman doctor?' Mrs Higgins screwed up her eyes as if she could not quite believe Annabel. She was too glamorous to be anything other than a shop mannequin, so people were often surprised to find out she was highly intelligent. It did not help that, by her behaviour, Annabel fostered the idea of being a bit of an airhead. I suspected that she liked people to underestimate her, so that they were more surprised and impressed when she showed just how clever she was.

'That's right,' said Annabel.

'Good. I'm glad I'm not the only one to get a medical degree. I once worked at St Bart's, you know. With the real Dr Watson.'

Annabel and I exchanged amused glances. 'I'm here to take a mould of your cabbage-stealer's boots,' I explained to Mrs Higgins. 'Could we have some boiling water please?'

We mixed the Plaster of Paris and I set about taking moulds of the footprints in Mrs Higgins's cabbage patch. 'You're sure you haven't walked in it since?' I asked as I waited for the plaster to set, not entirely sure that any answer Mrs Higgins gave me would be truthful.

'No. I was waiting for you to return. I thought you'd given up on me, my girl.'

'No, but I had important police work to do yesterday.'

'Yes, I heard you were selling raffle tickets for the policemen's ball. You didn't bring any my way.'

I felt as if I'd had my wrists slapped. Of course raffle tickets weren't as important to Mrs Higgins as her cabbages. 'I can bring some if you want some.'

'I'm not sure I want any now . . . Oh go on, then. Bring me ten. Mr Stanhope always provides a good hamper.'

'What do you know about him?' I asked, as I waited for the mould to set.

'He's a very private young man. His parents died quite a few years ago. Since then he's been mainly alone.'

'Rumour is he has a wife in a mental home,' said Annabel. 'Somewhere over towards Stockport.'

'Oh . . . ' I felt a little disappointed. Of course such a handsome man would have someone in his life. It was only natural. 'Oh well.'

'Not his wife,' said Mrs Higgins, shaking her head. 'His sister, Julia. She's about fifteen years older than he is. Mad as a hatter, she is. She once . . . ' Mrs Higgins suddenly gasped then clamped her lips shut as if she was about to say something that she should not have. It was unusual, as even in my early acquaintance with her I had realised that she did not always stop to think before speaking. 'Oh, well you don't want to know about all that, I'm sure.'

'We do,' we said together.

'No, you don't. Keep your mind on my cabbages.'

'Mrs Higgins,' I said, when it was clear that we were not going to get anything else about Leo's sister out of her, 'are you sure you didn't see anyone yesterday? I wondered if Mr Mapping's killer jumped off the dray and ran through your garden.'

'What does Sergeant Simmonds say?'

'He told me to shut up and sell raffle tickets.'

'He would. Well I daresay he wants to keep you safe.'

I wondered at that remark. I was a bit fed up with being treated like porcelain.

Once the mould had set there was little more for us to do, and the atmosphere had become rather strained. I looked at the mould, hoping it would tell me its secrets. The tread was large, suggesting a man's shoes or boots. I put it into the box on the back of the scooter.

'Well, I'd best be off,' I said. 'I'll let you know how I get on with it, Mrs Higgins.' Annabel went on her way to the hospital and Mrs Higgins started to tidy up her cabbage patch.

'Thank you,' the old woman said, as I revved up the scooter. 'Thank you for caring enough to do this. Oh I know you're after a murderer, but most people don't care about an old woman's vegetables, and I think you do care, a little bit, because you were going to take a mould before you thought of the murderer running through my cabbage patch. You're a good girl, Bobbie Blandford, and I think . . . yes, I think you're probably better off forgetting all that silly stuff I said yesterday when I read your fortune. Stay away from Leo Stanhope. It will only cause you pain in the end.'

4

With Mrs Higgins's words ringing in my ears, I went to the police station and straight to Sergeant Simmonds's office. The door was closed.

'He's busy,' said Peter Porter, who was working behind the counter, 'with Inspector Kirkham.'

'I need to talk to him about something. I took moulds from Mrs Higgins's garden. I think the footprints might have been left there by the person who killed Mr Mapping.' It did not occur to me that Porter was the last person I should trust. I did not like him, but I reasoned that it did not make him dishonest. Bear in mind I was young and inexperienced at the time, and I had not yet learned the benefit of keeping my theories to myself.

'How do you mean?' asked Porter, with a disbelieving look on his face.

'I think they hid in the dray, and then jumped off when it got nearer to the town. That's what caused the barrels to roll off.' I took the moulds out of the bag and put them onto the counter. 'I haven't had a proper look yet, but they look like large feet. A man's probably, and wearing heavy boots. Could be wellies.'

'Rubbish,' said Porter. 'That's a right daft leap.'

'Call it a hunch, Porter,' I said. 'Don't you ever have hunches?' Admittedly I had watched too many American crime films.

'Nah, only lunches.' He laughed at his own joke, poor as it was. 'Go and put the kettle on, there's a good girl. Then you can take over from me on the desk.'

'I'm not your employee, Porter,' I said, bristling. 'I take my orders from the sergeant.'

'Well the sergeant wants you on the desk, because we're going out to do some proper sleuthing. Here, it's on the rota.' Porter pointed to a sheet of paper that was pinned up behind the desk.

He was not lying. My name was down as manning the desk for the rest of the day. Two days at the station and I had spent most of them in the office. I wanted to be out solving crimes on the mean streets of Stony End. I did not know at the time if Stony End had anything approaching mean streets, but if they were there, I knew I was the girl to clean them up.

'But you can make a cuppa before you start. Marshall wants one too.'

DS Marshall was the plain-clothes detective who had been sent from a larger station to deal with the Mapping case. I had not had much chance to talk to him. He was in his late thirties, not bad-looking, but he had the unkempt look of a divorced man about him. He had been put in a small office next to the kitchenette. Well it was more of a broom cupboard really, but space was cramped in Stony End police station so we put him where we could. A desk had been crammed in there, and he had been given his own telephone line. The rest of us had to share one telephone and the radio.

Rather than arguing with Porter, I went to the kitchenette, knocking on Marshall's office as I passed. He opened the door with a phone pressed to his ear, talking to someone. He mouthed 'Sorry, busy', mimed drinking a cup of tea, and then shut the door in my face. I had no choice but to go and make the tea. Porter may not have been my senior, but Marshall was.

It took me about fifteen minutes by the time I had washed up all the dirty cups left over from the previous evening and made enough tea for the sarge, the visiting inspector, Marshall, the arresting sergeant and the three constables who were on duty in the station during the daytime. The other constable had been on the beat the day before, so I had not met him yet but I heard him come in as I made the tea.

'Hello,' he said with a friendly smile

when I carried the tray full of cups and biscuits into the reception area. He was a cuddly-looking man in his early fifties. He reminded me of Dixon of Dock Green. 'I'm Alf Norris.'

'Hello, Constable Norris. I'm Bobbie Blandford.' I put the tray on the counter.

'Ah, you're Robert's girl. Keeping up the family tradition, hey?'

'That's what I hope, Constable Norris.'

'Good, good. Now you call me Alf. My Greta has been looking forward to meeting you, so you'll have to come over for tea one day.'

I smiled broadly, feeling relief wash over me. Alf was the first person in the station to behave in a genuinely friendly manner towards me and over the years that followed I came to value his wisdom and advice. Despite being the oldest at the station, he seemed to have the most up-to-date views about women police. When I met his wife, Greta, I understood where he had got his modern view of women. She was a force to be reckoned with!

'Where's Constable Porter gone?' Alf asked.

'Said he had something important to share with the sarge.'

As if on cue, the door to Simmonds's office opened and a man stepped out whom I had never seen before, but immediately recognised from his uniform as the inspector. He was stationed at a larger town some miles away and did not visit Stony End very often. I saluted him just as I had been taught to do, but he was not looking at me.

'Good thinking, Porter. It's that sort of thing that'll make you a sergeant by the age of twenty-five. Get those moulds checked by the forensics people, Simmonds, and we might just catch our killer before the week is over.'

Porter and the sarge followed the inspector out. Porter was carrying the Plaster of Paris moulds that I had gone to all the trouble of taking.

'Oh . . . ' The inspector stopped,

realising I was there. 'So this is our new girl, is it? I've heard all about you, my girl,' he said. 'I also know why you had to leave your last job. You've been given a second chance here. Don't ruin it.' Without waiting for a reply from me — and I could not have spoken then, even if I wanted to — the inspector turned to the sarge. 'That's the problem with having pretty faces around. They put the men off their work.'

Porter grinned and I fought the compulsion to take the mould off him and smash it over his head. I wanted to protest and stick up for myself, but the inspector's insinuation had left me speechless.

The sarge looked annoyed, and I wondered if he had not known about my past indiscretion. He stared hard at me before seeing the inspector out of the building.

'I took those moulds,' I was finally able to say when both Simmonds and the inspector were out of earshot.

'But I took them to the sarge and the

inspector,' said Porter. 'So don't get your knickers in a twist, love. All that matters is that we catch the killer.' He winked at me again in the irritating way that he no doubt thought was endearing. He took the moulds — my moulds! — out to the back room, where Marshall was keeping most of the evidence.

'Let it go, lass,' Alf said kindly. 'There'll be a lot more of that, I'm afraid. Just save your breath for the big battles.'

'It's all a big battle when you're a woman,' I said as hot tears stung the back of my eyes. I fought them back, determined not to cry, not even in front of kindly Alf.

'It needn't be. Just do your job and don't give them any reason to discipline you. Then one day they'll realise they've got a good copper working with them.'

'How can you be sure of that, Alf?'

'I joined the police as a young man from the workhouse. You've no idea how I was looked down on at the time.

But I've worked hard and proved my worth. With a few hiccoughs along the way.'

'But . . . no offence, Alf, you're still a constable. I don't want to be a constable forever. I want to be a sergeant. I want to be a detective, though I doubt that'll ever happen in my lifetime.' Women could help with plain-clothes detective work in those days, but they could not hold a detective rank. I was young at the time and obviously could not see into the future. As far as I knew, it would never happen.

'I like being a constable,' Alf told me. 'I like being out there amongst the people who need us. Not stuck in an office, doing all the paperwork, until a juicy murder turns up. There's lots people like us, on the lowest rung, can do, that those further up can't. There's lots we can find out too.' Alf tapped the side of his nose. 'If people like you, Bobbie, they'll tell you anything. And people will like you. You're a nice girl. Not that I'd expect anything else of

Robert Blandford's daughter.'

'What makes you think I'm a nice girl?' I asked. 'You heard what the inspector said.'

'Do you know what they say about Stony End, lass?'

'What?'

'Stony End is the place that'll take you in when no one else will. We've all got our secrets here. We've all made our mistakes. It's not a bad place to spend purgatory. Me and Greta have got our own little prefab up on the estate and we love it here. I don't miss the city at all. Never mind what the inspector said. No one cares about your past.'

'Oh I think Porter is very interested.'

'Porter is an idiot, but he's no different. He's got his reasons for being here. Marshall out there likes the pop a bit too much, which is why we always get him instead of one of the better detectives.'

'And Simmonds?'

'Never mind my reasons,' said a curt voice from the door.

I swallowed hard. I had not heard the sarge coming back. 'Sorry, Sarge,' I mumbled.

'Forget it,' said Simmonds. 'I know it was you who took the moulds, Blandford, and I'll make sure it's noted.'

'You knew?' I wondered why he had not said so.

'These station walls are very thin and your voice carries a bit. I heard you talking about it when you came in. So did the inspector for that matter, but if you look for praise from him, you won't get it. And it's not just you, Blandford. None of us will. He's one of those bureaucrats who want all police services centralised. He's been trying to close this station for years and I won't give him a good reason. Not while Stony End needs us. So do as Alf here says. Forget about what happened in the past. Just do your job well. At least well enough so that blithering idiot hasn't got an excuse to shut us down.'

'Yes, Sarge.' I felt relief wash over me. I also felt as if I had been given something to fight for. Simmonds, as brusque as he behaved, seemed to believe in me. I guessed that he also believed in Porter, or the lad would not be here, though I could not see why. 'I won't let you down, I promise.'

'Glad to hear it. Now, you're on the desk all day today. Just log any complaints that come in, either by phone or in person, and arrange for Alf to go and see them if you think they need a follow-up. If anything comes over the radio, it'll be an emergency so you let me know.'

'Yes, Sarge. I used to work as a receptionist in a hotel.'

'Good, then you know what you're doing.'

Half an hour later, I began to wonder if that was true. At the hotel where I worked I had experienced nuisance calls, but nothing like I had to deal with at the station.

'No, I do not wear red frilly knickers, but I'm sure your mother would be very interested to know you're asking,' I remember saying to one particularly annoying boy on the telephone . . . 'I'm sorry, madam, I don't know why you can get ITV but not BBC on your television. Perhaps you need to tune BBC in . . . No, I'm sorry, I cannot come around and do it for you.' . . . 'If you think the drains smell, Miss Cartwright, perhaps you would be better calling a plumber than the police station. No, I'm sorry, I don't have the number of a plumber to hand.' It seemed that all my training had been wasted. I had expected to solve crimes and protect the public from the wicked. It turned out that I might as well have worked for directory enquiries.

Then there were those who came in wanting to drop their neighbours in it for some perceived crime. 'I'm telling you, he's a spy,' said one harassed-looking woman in her thirties pushing a baby in a pram and carrying a toddler in her arms.

'What makes you think he's a spy?' I asked. I must admit I got a little bit excited. The war was not that long ago and some of the old paranoia about fifth-columnists still lingered. It was said that not all of them had returned home and that they were 'sleeping', awaiting the next big war.

'He's got a telescope and he's always looking through it. I think he's trying to steal secrets off the NHS. Always pointing it at the hospital, up the hill.'

'Maybe he's an astronomer.'

'Ah, see, I thought that. But when I asked him to tell me my horoscope, he didn't have a clue what I was talking about.'

'That's an astrologer.'

'It's the same thing, isn't it?'

'Erm . . . no, it isn't. I'll ask Constable Norris to call around and see you,' I promised.

When Alf dropped in for a cuppa halfway through his beat and I told him all about it, he grinned. 'That'll be Mr Wilson. He's not an astronomer, astrologer or spy. But I will call around and have a word with him. I've had to warn him before.'

'Why, Alf?'

'Because he's not trying to steal secrets off the hospital, unless it's what the nurses are wearing. He's a peeping Tom.'

I groaned. 'Now why didn't that occur to me? I'm so bored, I actually wanted him to be a spy.'

'That's Stony End for you. Still, he's harmless enough.'

I wanted to go into all the theories I'd read about how men who started off as peeping Toms or flashers often went on to make serious attacks on women, but I liked Alf, so I saved him the lecture. I also appreciated that a word from the kindly Alf might do the trick, whereas to go to Wilson all guns a-blazing, accusing him of perversion, might actually tip him over the edge to becoming a full-blown sex offender.

It was the afternoon when a well-dressed woman in her late thirties came into the station. I had not seen her before, but she was clearly someone of great importance in the area. She had a cold air about her and hair that was lacquered so well that if anyone had hit it, they would have broken their hand. She was accompanied by a man of similar age. He was one of those bland good-looking types, with a slightly weak mouth but nice eyes.

'I am Gloria Mapping and this is Kenneth Truman. We have an appointment to see Detective Sergeant Marshall.'

'Are you Mr Mapping's daughter? I am very sorry for your loss,' I said, with all the sympathy and professionalism I could muster. I was not yet used to dealing with death, but I knew that one of my duties would often be to inform relatives. I still wondered why I had not been allowed to inform Miss Mapping of her father's death. 'I'll fetch DS Marshall immediately.'

'Thank you.'

Marshall came through and took Miss Mapping and Mr Truman through to his office. I followed them through. That was another duty, being present when women were being questioned. I waited just inside the door of the tiny office.

'Does she have to stay?' asked Gloria Mapping.

'It's customary to have a WPC present when women are being questioned,' said DS Marshall.

'I was not aware I was being questioned, DS Marshall. Inspector Kirkham said I only had to attend to clear up some of the business pertaining to my father's death.'

'Of course,' said Marshall, his eyes looking wary at the sound of Inspector Kirkham's name. 'But I'm sure the inspector would prefer we follow procedure.'

'Mr Truman is a solicitor, so he can look after my interests. Tell her to go. I don't want her in the room. I'm quite willing to contact Inspector Kirkham and bring this up with him. He and my father were great friends, you know.'

Marshall had the grace to look at me apologetically. 'You may go, WPC Blandford,' he said. 'We do need someone on the desk after all.'

Gloria Mapping turned around and glared at me. 'That will be all,' she said, dismissing me as if I were her maid. I had no choice but to leave the room, even though I felt procedure was not being followed and that I was taking my orders from Gloria Mapping rather than DS Marshall.

I must admit I was dying to know what was being said, so I decided that the counter could be left unattended just for a short while as I made more tea. After all, that was what everyone expected me to do and as the sarge said, the walls in the police station were rather thin.

Unfortunately I could only hear a low murmur from Marshall's office when I was in the kitchen. The noise from the kettle boiling did not help. Then I heard the phone ring and dashed back through to the counter, not wanting to be caught off my post. I was only vaguely aware of someone walking into the station as I picked up the phone only to find it was that pesky child again.

'Look, if you don't behave, I will tell your mother. Clearly you are off school today, and it isn't the school holidays, so it shouldn't be too hard to track you down. Now for the last time my knickers are neither red and frilly nor blue and frilly.'

'Thank you for letting me know,' said a deep voice on the other side of the counter. I looked up to see Leo Stanhope standing there.

I dropped the phone back in its cradle with a clatter. 'Hello, how may I help you?' I asked formally.

'I wanted to apologise for yesterday.'

'There's no need really.'

'Yes, there is. I was very rude to you and you'd done nothing to deserve it. It's just that your name caught me off guard.'

'My name?'

'Yes. It's hard to explain here. I wondered whether you'd like to meet me tonight for a drink in the Cunning Woman.'

'I'm not sure that's allowed.'

'You're not allowed to drink?'

'I mean I don't think I'm allowed to fraternise with . . . ' I almost said 'a suspect', but it was only in my mind he was a suspect, and that had more to do with me feeling awkward in his handsome presence than any real idea of him being a murderer. 'With the public.'

'So you're not allowed to date anyone outside of the police force? Ever? Because basically, we're all the public.'

'Actually I'm not supposed to fraternise with workmates. Not that there's much chance of that. Alf Norris is an angel, but he's in his fifties and married. The sarge is okay, but well, he's a bit old. Marshall is a strange one. As for Porter . . . ' I scoffed.

'After all that, I dread to think why you're turning me down. Apart from me being a member of the public.'

'I don't know. I just . . . Mrs Higgins said you'd be bad for me. Then again, she is a pathological liar and possibly quite mad.'

'I think she's actually quite shrewd. I probably would be bad for you. In fact, it's taken me since yesterday to pluck up courage to ask you out. But faint hearts and fair maidens and all that.' He turned to go, but half-turned back. 'I'm sure you could find a dozen reasons not to go out with me, but just in case you discard them all, and decide I'm worth taking a chance on, I'll be in the Cunning Woman at seven o'clock. Nursing my broken heart.' His eyes twinkled.

★ ★ ★

'What are you going to do?' asked Annabel when I arrived back at the cottage at around six thirty and told my new friend about Leo's offer. She followed me to my bedroom and perched on the bed. 'Are you going?'

'I can't decide. I made a huge mistake before, Annabel, and it cost me my job. I can't afford to make another mistake.'

'What happened? I know you said you left under a cloud but you didn't say what.'

I sighed and sat down at the dressing table, resting my head in my hands. 'I'd been at the hotel about eighteen months when I became involved with one of the waiters. He was Italian and very gorgeous. He had a bad reputation, but I was young and stupid and it only made him seem more attractive. He had this James Dean thing going for him. What I didn't know was that unlike James Dean, my fella had a wife and children back in Italy. We were found out and it was one of the darkest moments of my life, for lots of reasons. When word got out the manager called us in and hauled us over the coals, but said that he — the Italian — was too important to lose. So I would have to go. The manager also told me about the wife and children. That was the first I knew of them. At the same time they were doing a recruiting drive for women police officers and it seemed like a good way out. So here I am. See, it's not just going on a date with Leo that's the problem. It's that if anything comes of it, he'll have to know what happened before. I'm damaged goods, Annabel.'

'Come on, this is 1960. No one thinks like that anymore. And if Leo Stanhope does, he's not worth having.'

'Oh, there speaks a fashionable girl from London. We're in Derbyshire, Annabel. Some of these towns still operate on medieval standards.'

'So that's it? You're going to become a nun?'

'Practically. Though I hear the wimple is a bit scratchy.'

'Do you want to see him?'

I nodded. 'Oh yes. He's gorgeous, and I think there's something quite dark about him. Just my type in fact. Which probably means he does have a mad wife in an asylum. She probably shares a padded cell with his sister.'

I grinned to show I was joking, but in reality there was little humour in it. 'No one will believe it,' I continued. 'But I'm a good girl really. I wouldn't have given myself to the Italian if I hadn't been so sure I was in love at the time. I thought we'd be married and until then I'd been saving myself until I married.' I laughed, with more humour that time. 'See how contrary I am? I tell myself I want James Dean and a bit of danger, but really I want the cottage with roses around the door, the picket fence and the two point four children. I don't know where Leo Stanhope will fit into all that.' I looked at the clock on the wall. It was five to seven. 'Have you got a dress I can borrow?' I asked Annabel. 'You have such lovely clothes and mine are all so tomboyish.' Out of uniform I lived in pedal pushers and sweaters.

'Okay, but promise me that at least for this first date you won't mention cottages or picket fences. And definitely avoid the two point four children!'

'Really?' I quipped. 'I was going to open the conversation with all that.'

5

Halfway to the pub I stopped to wonder what on earth I was doing. I'd only just made one huge mistake with a romance, and it should have made me wary. Yet here I was, going headlong into something new with Leo Stanhope. That night I was full of hope for the future.

I'd only been in the police force a couple of days, and whilst I'd read about all the bad stuff in Moriarty's manual, I had not even come close to experiencing it. It was hard to believe there was darkness in Stony End. Even Mapping's murder had a strangely humorous twist to it, and I'd heard lots of the townspeople joking about 'what a way to go' when it was reported that Mapping had died in a vat of ale.

On the way to the pub to meet a

handsome man, and despite my misgivings about going on a date with him, I felt that I ruled the world. Put it down to me being young and stupid. Better still, just call me a cock-eyed optimist, like Mitzi Gaynor in *South Pacific*. Despite my experience with the Italian, I still wanted to believe in the good things in the world, though over the months and years that followed, my youthful optimism would be tested to the limit.

'You came!' Leo said, a bit redundantly, when I entered the pub. It was quarter past seven, so I could have forgiven him for giving up and going home.

'Yes,' I said, 'though I probably shouldn't have.' All the locals had stopped what they were doing to look at me. Some of them already knew I was the new policewoman, because I'd seen them around the station, but others did not. Either way, they all seemed interested in this newcomer who had walked into their midst.

'Let me get you a drink and you can tell me why.' He led me to a small table near to the fire, which was lit. 'What do you want?'

'A gin and tonic, please.' I had no idea what gin and tonic tasted like, as it was a drink I associated with my mother and my maiden aunts, but I thought it made me sound sophisticated.

'Make that two,' Leo said to the barmaid. 'Can I get you anything else? Crisps or nuts? Or a meat pie?'

'Erm . . . '

'I'm starving, you see, so I could do with a pie or something. I've had three deliveries today, all of them difficult.'

'Don't let me stop you.' I could not have eaten a thing. Until then, because of the circumstances of our meetings, I had seen him as a creature way above me. But to hear him talk about being hungry and wanting a meat pie made him seem more human. And that was more dangerous, because it made him seem attainable, which led to its own set of fears.

I drank my gin and tonic — which I had to admit was not bad — whilst he ate a pie. 'It must be wonderful seeing new life come into the world,' I said. 'We had training for it but I'm not sure it has prepared me.'

'Nothing can, but nature knows what to do, so there's no need to worry,' said Leo, swallowing the last of his pie and wiping his mouth with a napkin. 'Sometimes there are difficulties and that's when you call me.'

'I'll remember that.'

'I'm glad you came, Bobbie. I can call you Bobbie, can't I?'

'Yes, of course.'

'I like it. It suits you.' He smiled that wonderful smile.

'It's better than Roberta. Though I don't mind being named after my dad. He was very brave.'

For some reason, Leo's smile dropped. 'I'm sorry about what happened to him.' I did not realise it then, but later I got to thinking that he was apologising personally, and not just in the general way that people do when they hear that someone has died. I just did not know why.

'It's a long time ago now. There's so much I don't know,' I said. 'I didn't even know till last night that I'd lived in Stony End as a child. You'd have been little too, so I don't suppose you remember us.'

'I was thirteen,' he said, 'when your father died.'

'So you do know about it?'

'Of course.' He seemed to be choosing his words carefully. 'A policeman dying on the beat is something that one does remember. Especially in a little place like Stony End.'

'Did you know my dad at all? It's just that no one tells me that much. Of course Mum adored him, and my brother, who was about the same age as you when it happened, also has memories. But I don't, and I so want to.'

'Bobbie,' Leo said, in a gentle voice, 'sometimes things are better left in the past.'

'That's easy for someone who's never lost someone important to say . . . ' I stopped suddenly. 'I'm sorry, that was unfair. I remember you telling me that you lost your parents not long ago. But you did at least know them.'

'I know they had a very unhappy life for a long time,' he said, his eyes dark with pain.

'I'm sorry.'

He took a deep breath and appeared to cheer up. 'But as I said, let the past go, and let's think of the future. I'm glad you're here, in Stony End. I'm glad to see you've grown up into a beautiful and self-assured young woman.' I hardly knew where to look. No one, not even the flirty Italian, had ever called me beautiful. Though to be fair, as he did most of his flirting in Italian, he might have said it and I had not realised. But I definitely noticed with Leo Stanhope.

110

'Here's to surviving,' I said, raising my glass. Only by then it was empty so I was left feeling a bit daft.

'Time for another round,' said Leo, with a grin.

'Let me,' I said. After all I was an independent woman, and it was time I learned how to order my own drink.

'No. My treat. Besides,' he said, lowering his voice, 'I'm afraid that if a young lady went to the bar in Stony End, it would create a scandal. They're a bit behind the times here.'

I liked how he managed to be chivalrous without making me feel like a weak and feeble woman. It was other people and their attitudes we had to contend with.

Okay, I admit I was already falling a little bit in love with him, but it was in a fun way. He was very handsome and a doctor. My mother would certainly approve. For me he was part of my growing up and becoming more independent. The Italian had been a stupid mistake, but I had become a career

woman and could have mature relationships with men without feeling guilty
about it.

Oh it all seemed so easy that first
night, and I thought I had it under
control. We chatted until closing time
about our favourite music, our favourite
films and books, and then he walked
me home.

'Oh no, it's that song again!' I
groaned, as we reached the cottage. The
Drifters' 'Save the Last Dance for Me'
was blaring f the neighbour's
house.

'I like it,' said Leo.

'So do I,' I agreed quickly. 'But she
does play it rather a lot.'

'She was Mapping's secretary, wasn't
she?'

'Yes, that's right. She's supposed to
be heartbroken over his death.'

'She's about the only one who is.'

'What did you know about him?'

'He was not a good man. He conned
my parents out of their business, at a
time in their lives when they were

vulnerable. He's done the same to others too.'

'So you have a motive,' I said.

'Yes, but I also have an alibi for the time he was found dead.'

'Oh?'

'Yes, and I shall give it to the police if they ever ask me.' He clearly was not going to tell me what it was.

'I'm the police,' I reminded him, as gently as I could.

'Do you really think I'm a murderer, Bobbie?' We were by the garden gate and he was looking down at me, his face in shadow.

'I . . . no, perhaps not. It is hard to believe that a man who saves lives and brings babies into the world can take lives.'

'Dr Crippen would have been glad to hear you say it,' Leo said. I did not see his wicked grin clearly, but I felt the force of it.

'Were you with a woman? Is that it? Because I won't be shocked or upset. After all, I didn't know you then. Not that it's any of my business now. I mean we're not . . . we haven't . . . '

'I was with a woman, yes.'

Okay, maybe I was a little upset about it, but I think I hid it well. 'Best say good night then,' I tried to say as breezily as I could.

'I have shocked you.'

'No, of course not,' I demurred. 'I'm not exactly as pure as the driven snow myself.'

'Oh.' I think it was his turn to be upset, but I felt glad to have made a point. 'I had an affair with an Italian.' Why I blurted that out, I'll never know. I suppose I wanted to get my own back on him and also to show him that I was every bit as sophisticated as he was. 'He was married. Only I didn't know that at the time.'

'That must have hurt very much.'

'Yes, it did.' Why was he being so understanding? I think I'd have preferred him to show some jealousy. 'Is your friend married? Is that it?'

'No. It's not a friend. It's my sister.'

'What?' That was not the way I expected things to go and some of the stuff I'd read in *Moriarty's Police Law* ran through my head. Surely not . . . ?

'I'm not having an affair with my sister, Bobbie.' Leo laughed softly. 'I was visiting her. She's not very well.'

'Then why couldn't you have just told me that? Why make such a big secret of it?'

'It's hard to explain. One day you'll understand why I didn't bring her up in conversation, and by then I hope you'll know me — care about me — well enough to forgive me.'

'And you let me blurt that stuff out about the Italian! I'd best go in before your opinion of me falls any further.' I went to open the gate, and he put his hand over mine to stop me. The song was still playing, and it seemed to resonate in the evening air.

'My opinion of you could not be any higher than it is, Bobbie. I promise you that. I think you're a wonderful girl.'

'Oh.' I looked up at him, his face still

shadowed, because the street light was behind him. Would he kiss me? Should I let him on a first date? He might think I was easy. He had good reason to after what I'd told him about the Italian. But how could I prove to him that I was not easy if I let him kiss me too soon? Despite my self-styled sophistication, I felt like a sixteen-year-old again.

'Do you know what the singer is saying?' he asked.

'I think so . . . '

'He's saying that he doesn't care what other men the girl smiles at or dances with. All he cares about is that he's the one she goes home with. It doesn't matter what you've done before in your life. All I care about now is your future and whether I have a part in it.'

In that he eventually proved to be a much better person than I was, but moved by the simple honesty of his words, I quickly kissed him on the cheek. 'Thank you. I really appreciate that.'

Before he could say anything else, I ran into the cottage and shut the door, resisting the urge to give a squeal of delight as I ran up the stairs to bed.

6

Between Leo's shifts at the hospital and his local practice, and my shifts as a policewoman, our times together were very rare, but very precious. We always met in the pub, and I was never invited to his house, but I figured that would take time. Our snatched moments gave us little time to discuss what really mattered, so it is not surprising that when I learned the truth, it was shocking.

I should have known something was wrong, because one morning the sarge called me in. 'I hear you've been seeing Dr Stanhope,' he said.

'That's right, Sarge.'

'I see.'

'Is there a problem, Sarge?'

He looked at me for a long time, and not for the first time I wondered if he was going to be difficult. He had shown no romantic interest in me that I could discern. Yet I did sense he was interested in me, for reasons I could not fathom. In those days, senior policemen could become involved in the romances of their underlings. Policemen had to ask permission to marry, and even then they could only marry a woman who was deemed suitable by the chief constable.

'Has he told you about his sister Julia?'

'About how she's in a mental home? Yes, Sarge. You really don't believe in all this hereditary stuff, do you? Because it doesn't bother me.'

'No, no, of course not. As long as you know. Just be careful, that's all.'

'Dr Stanhope is respectable enough, Sarge.'

'Yes, he's a good man ... I just needed to warn you, that's all.' The Sarge looked at a loss as to what to say next. He was not usually a man to mince his words.

Over the weeks and months that

followed my first date with Leo, I learned more about my police duties, including going out on the beat with Alf Norris, which was one of my favourite parts of policing. I learned where all the different 'points' were. These were telephone boxes, either police-type (recognisable to many as a Tardis, since *Doctor Who* started in 1963) or the old red telephone boxes that are now a national icon. Our walks were timed so that we reached certain points at certain times. I got to know people and they got to know me. I also learned about the 'good' parts of Stony End and the 'bad' parts. That is, the areas where prostitutes might linger — usually around the back of the pub on pay day or the town hall steps. Whether that was to catch the councillors on their way home with their expenses I did not know. But the girls on the game were good-natured, and it was possible to strike up a friendship with them, albeit one with strict boundaries. The older women always took care of the younger girls.

'We don't want them going off to London,' one of the older prostitutes, Pearl, told me one night. 'They're not very well treated down there.'

There were also public lavatories where the homeless sheltered. It was one of my jobs to move them on to hostels or missions if I could.

'But if they're dry and comfortable, let them be, lass,' Alf Norris told me. 'God knows the poor souls don't have anywhere else to go.'

At first I was horrified, both by the prostitutes and the homeless people. I saw it as my job to clean up the streets and felt it wrong to let such people clutter up the Stony End loos at night. Forgive me. I was young at the time and saw life in black and white terms, much of it due to my upbringing. You either worked hard and did well, or you failed at life and fell into wickedness. There was no middle ground.

Then I met Verity.

I was on the evening shift and

finishing off my rounds when I found her sitting in one of the cubicles in the public loos that were situated in a dank cellar underneath the high street. She was wrapped up in an old blanket, but her clothing looked well made. At the time I put her age at about fourteen, which made her a minor and a runaway, and definitely in need of my care. I must admit to feeling a bit pleased with myself about it. This was what I had been brought into the police force to do. The power went to my head.

'Now, little one,' I said to her in patronising tones, forgetting all I had read in my manuals about how to deal with such a situation. 'Let's get you out of here and into a hostel, then we can ring your mum and get her to take you home. Won't that be nice?' All I saw was a lost child happily reunited with her mother, with me in centre place as the heroine who had brought this to fruition.

She answered by rushing past me and

up the stairs out into the night. I gave chase, but by the time I was at the top of the stairs, she had disappeared. I was late home that night as I spent another hour looking for her to no avail.

The following night I looked for her as I walked the streets. I asked Alf Norris to look for her on his beat and to let me know immediately he found her. I even asked Pearl and the other girls on the town hall steps if they'd look out for her.

'We will and we'll get in touch with you straight away,' Pearl agreed. I must have looked doubtful. 'If she's under-age, we don't want her here,' Pearl told me then. 'We're all adults and can make up our own minds. We don't encourage kids into this job. We'll do our best to put her off, don't you worry.'

I had just reached the police box on the common at around nine o'clock when the phone rang. 'I've found your girl,' said Alf. 'We're in the caff on the high street.'

I made my way there as quickly as

possible, only slowing my steps as I drew nearer. I did not want to alarm her again. I was glad really that she had not been found by Pearl first, as the elderly lady of the night might well have frightened the girl away so that she left Stony End for good.

The café had been decorated in the style of an American diner, with plastic-topped, chrome-rimmed tables. There was a jukebox in the corner at which stood two teddy boys and their girlfriends. One lad wore a purple drape suit edged with a black collar and cuffs, and a thin tie. On his feet were the huge shoes known as brothel creepers. The other lad wore a black drape with red collar and cuffs. His shoes were red to match the trim of his garments. The girls, identical twins, were both dressed in blue satin full-circle skirts, with a tight top and a jaunty scarf around their necks. They looked up when I walked in, but then went back to choosing their music. There was some good-natured debate going on. The girls wanted to listen to 'Are You Lonesome Tonight?' by Elvis Presley, whilst the boys wanted to listen to a Buddy Holly song, 'Not Fade Away'.

'I can't be doing with that Elvis,' said one of the boys. 'He's gone soft since his Sun Record years. You mark my words, we'll have forgotten him by this time next year.'

'I won't,' said one of the twins, sighing happily. 'I'm going to marry him.'

'Good, 'cause you'll not be marrying me,' said the lad in the black drape.

'You don't mean that, Stan. Do you?'

'Well you can't marry me if you're marrying Elvis, can you, Shirley?'

'Depends who asks me first,' Shirley said, winking at her twin. 'What do you reckon, Joan?'

'I'm going to marry Frankie Vaughan.'

The foursome's youthful frivolity formed a stark contrast to the young girl I had come to see. She played down her looks with drab clothing and unkempt hair.

'Hello,' I said, sitting opposite the girl. 'I'm WPC Blandford. What's your name?'

Alf had bought her a Knickerbocker Glory, which she ate whilst looking at me over the rim, her eyes gleaming with distrust. 'Are You Lonesome Tonight?' struck up on the jukebox, showing that the girls had won their argument.

'I'm sorry I frightened you off yesterday,' I said. 'I didn't mean to. I just thought your mum might be worried.'

'She won't be,' the girl said between slurps.

'This is Verity,' Alf informed me. 'She's eighteen.' Something in his voice told me that he did not believe that any more than I did, but if that was what Verity had said, it would be hard to disprove until we had heard back from the missing persons department.

'Oh. You look much younger. Can I ask why you're sleeping rough, Verity?' I looked to Alf for affirmation. Was I asking the right questions? 'I mean apart from you having nowhere to go. Do you . . . is there anyone you would like us to call?'

She shook her head. 'I can't go back there.'

'Did someone hurt you?'

Verity looked down at her Knickerbocker Glory and did not answer. She never did answer that question with specifics, but it was clear that sometime in the past she had been frightened badly. Every time the café door opened, she jumped as if fearing an attack from somewhere.

'We'd like to help you. It can't be very nice, sleeping on the streets.'

'It's better here than in the city,' she whispered. 'It was awful there.' Her whole body shuddered and I dreaded to think what she had been through, both in the city and in the home that she did not see as a refuge.

'But there are better places to sleep than those smelly old loos,' I said.

'There's a hostel nearby that takes young girls who don't have a home to go to.'

'I've been in one, and they spend all the time telling you that you're a sinner. Even if things are not your fault. They tell you that if bad happens to you, it's because you've done something to deserve it.'

'Mrs Watson at the hostel is not like that,' Alf assured her. 'She's a nice lady. In fact, she spent some time on the streets herself a good few years back, so she knows what it's like.'

'We could take you there and if you don't like it, you don't have to stay,' I pitched in, earning a look of admiration from Alf. It would give us more time to find out the truth about her.

As we left to take Verity to the hostel, 'Not Fade Away' started on the jukebox and I wished I could have stayed to listen. Part of me wanted to be like the carefree twins, and I wished Verity could be the same. As we walked, I tried to gently coax information about her life from her.

'Is your mum nice?' she asked me suddenly.

'Yes. Most of the time. I mean she can be a bit clingy and snobbish, but she's a good woman with a good heart. Isn't your mum?'

'Sometimes. When I'm doing what she wants me to do.'

There was something ominous about the way Verity said that. I must admit my mind ran to all sorts of dark thoughts. 'Is that why you ran away?'

Verity nodded. 'Yes. I loved her all the time but she only loved me if I was doing what she said. When I have children I shall love and protect them no matter what.'

'So your mum had a boyfriend then?' I coaxed gently.

'Not just the one. And they were all the same.'

If Verity did anything, it was to make me think differently about my own mum. Yes, she was overprotective, but mothers were supposed to protect their children. Verity's mother appeared to have failed in that regard. She also made me see homeless people differently, and by extension the girls on the town hall steps. They were not people who had failed at life. They were people whom life had failed.

'Do you not have any aunts or uncles who might take you in?' I asked.

'None of them will have anything to do with us. Anyway, they'd just tell Mum where I was. I never want to see her again.'

Mrs Watson at the hostel was a motherly woman in her fifties. She cooed and fussed over Verity, but in a non-threatening way. I saw the girl visibly relax in her presence. Only when Verity realised she would have to share a room with others did she balk.

'I'd prefer my own room,' she said.

'I know, dear,' said Mrs Watson, 'and I wish I could do that for all of you, but it's not possible. There are so many people to help. But the men's dormitories are in the other wing and the door between them is locked. There's an orderly — a nice girl she is, used to be on the streets herself — on that door all night. You're not the only one who comes here afraid, you see, and we will take care of you.'

Verity reluctantly agreed to stay there on those terms, but I could see she was not very happy. We were led to a common room where young people sat around a television watching *Hancock's Half Hour*. They were laughing, yet there was something empty about their laughter. As if they were afraid of being happy. I did not want to leave Verity there, but we had no choice.

By the time we found out that she was not yet sixteen, she had already run away again. 'We couldn't stop her,' Mrs Watson said regretfully when I called into the hostel the next day. 'If these girls get it in their minds to go, there's nothing we can do.'

I looked for Verity every time I was on the beat after that, but it seemed she had left Stony End. For a while I wondered what had happened to her, but other cases came and went, and I'm sorry to say that I forgot about her. She became just another in a sea of lonely souls that we dealt with on a regular basis.

Those brought up on series like *CSI* and various cop shows will think that the hunt for Mapping's murder moved very slowly, but that's how it was in those days. Unless the killer was someone who had been found on the scene, tracking down the culprit was not as easy as the television shows make it appear. DNA had been discovered, but its uses in forensics were a long way off. Fingerprints might have helped, had Mr Mapping not been found dead in a factory used by dozens of workers and daily visitors. His death became something of a curiosity, especially given the darkly comical nature of it, with him falling into a vat of beer, but the clues were few and far between. I tentatively asked about the moulds with the shoe prints, only to be told that nothing definite had been found out about them. The sarge still insisted I keep out of it, giving me the less important jobs to do in the station.

'Do you know, Sarge,' I said to him one morning when I was put on desk duty once again, 'some women police are sent for CID training?'

'Not within a few months of joining the force, they're not,' he said. 'You're still on probation.'

'But maybe I could help out with the Mapping case.'

'No, but you can put the files into the cold cases folder.' Cold cases were those that had not been solved.

'Are there many of those? Cold cases? I'd love to get a look at them.'

'Maybe I'll give you the chance to. Some of the others work on them in their spare time. It would be something for you to practise on, I suppose, without causing too much chaos.' I almost thanked him cheekily for the vote of confidence, but realised that things were going my way so kept quiet.

'Yes, all right, Blandford. Do your desk duty today, and then tomorrow I'll put you on cold cases. It might be a good idea to get a fresh eye on them.'

I had visions of solving all the cases and proving that I was the best thing to happen to female detection since Miss Marple. Clearly the only thing Stony End police station had been lacking was me.

I had a day on the desk to get through first. I had also finally been pinned down to attending Alf Norris's house for tea so I could meet his wife, Greta. It meant not seeing Leo on a rare evening we both had free, which was one reason I had put it off so long. But truth be known, I was a bit afraid of Greta Norris's reputation. She had been a police wife for many years, and was quite formidable, according to the sarge. 'Even I stand to attention when Mrs Norris enters a room,' he told me.

As it turned out, Greta was far less threatening to me than Inspector Kirkham. He arrived in the afternoon whilst the sarge was out on business. I stood to attention, as was proper, and showed him into the sarge's room. Peter Porter, whom I had managed to avoid for quite a while, was hovering around the waiting room as if he had been expecting the inspector's visit.

'Come on in, WPC Blandsome,' said Inspector Kirkham.

'It's Blandford, sir,' I said.

'Is it, now? You come in too, Porter. Shut the door behind you, there's a good lad.'

I knew something was wrong when the door slammed shut behind me. 'Now, Blandford, I hear that the proper niceties aren't being adhered to in this station.'

'I'm afraid I don't know what you mean, sir. If there is a problem with my work, the sarge hasn't said so.'

'Oh your work is exemplary, according to the reports, if a little uninspiring.'

That hurt. I knew I was only a probationer, but I had hoped to shine a little more in police despatches. I was fast coming to the conclusion that my enthusiasm outstripped my abilities.

'No, lass, I'm talking about your proper initiation ceremony. You can't be a member of the police force unless you are properly initiated, and Porter here tells me that no one has done it.'

'I don't know what you mean, sir,' I said, hating myself for repeating what I had already said. I did have an inkling then what he meant. I had heard the stories, but I put them down to urban legends; the sort of silly tales people told newbies to frighten them.

For the first time I realised that the inspector had been playing with some rubber stamps on the sarge's desk. They were either marked with dates, for filing, or said 'Vermin' or 'Unfit for Human Consumption'. The latter were used when we checked on sanitary conditions in local businesses and farms.

'Since Porter is also new, we'll let him do the honours. Initiate you both, eh?'

'No, sir.' I stood proudly, determined I was not going to be drawn into such silly games.

'Now, lass, don't be a spoilsport. You need a sense of humour in this game.' The inspector handed a stamp to Porter. At the same time, I made for the door. 'Or you could find your probation coming to a very sudden end. One word from me . . . '

I could not believe he was doing such a thing. Despite all his talk of it being a joke, there was something sinister about his behaviour. As if he was putting me in my place.

'You can choose where,' he said, with an ugly grin. 'Either on your chest or just above your stockings.' He had started walking towards me.

'Neither,' I said, feeling my knees tremble. 'I choose neither. I won't be humiliated like this . . . sir.'

At that, he grabbed my arm. 'Just do it, lad. On her leg will do.' Kirkham's hand reached to the hem of my skirt.

'No!' I called. As police we would

never allow other women to be assaulted in such a way, yet it was treated as part of the game and one was supposed to play it.

Just when I thought Porter would stamp my upper leg with 'Vermin', and I would lose all dignity, the door to the office flew open. I thought it was the sarge returning, but it was Leo. His face was dark with rage.

I felt humiliation swallow me whole then at the thought of how it must look to him, with one man holding me whilst the other was going to mark me as vermin. I fled the office in tears and went to lock myself in the toilets, filled with shame and self-loathing. I believed that if I had not had a reputation as a girl who had once had an affair with a married man, they would not have dared to humiliate me in such a way.

'Bobbie . . . ' Leo knocked on the door five minutes later. 'Bobbie, sweetheart, it's all right. It's not your fault.'

'I know that!'

'What I mean is that I know you're

going to be worrying about what I think, but I could see what happened. I've got eyes in my head. What the inspector and Porter tried to do was outrageous.'

'He'll get me thrown off the force now. I should have just let it happen. Other girls say they did, and they were left alone then. Now I'll never be left alone.'

'No, you shouldn't have let him do it. Men do things like that to attempt ownership of women and they only do that when they feel threatened.'

He finally coaxed me out of the loos and gave me a hug. 'I'll lose my job,' I sobbed against his shoulder.

'Then you'll get another one. Somewhere they treat you with dignity. But if I know Sergeant Simmonds, he won't be happy about this.'

'How do you know? He might have joined in if he'd been here.' Even as I said it, I knew it was not true. Alf Norris would not have joined in either. The inspector was a bully and Porter was weak and stupid, doing whatever he thought would please 'the boss'. I truly hated him then. More than that, I hated myself for being so powerless against them. If Leo had not turned up, I would not have been able to stop them, yet I was a policewoman. I had been trained in ju-jitsu. I should have been able to defend myself. Not that it was advisable to use martial arts against one's fellow officers.

I had been lulled into a false sense of security at Stony End police station. When the sarge was there I was treated with respect, even if Porter verged on the side of belligerence most of the time. Alf Norris looked upon me as a daughter figure, so would not have dreamed of being so personal. The officers on the opposite shifts treated me as a bit of a curiosity, but were never unkind. It was almost as if Kirkham had been waiting until I truly settled in.

'Oh,' I said, looking at my watch as Leo held me close. I gulped back a sob.

'I have to go to Alf's for tea.'

'Are you all right now?'

'Yes, I think so.'

'Don't worry about anything. I'll tell Sergeant Simmonds what I saw.'

'Thank you.' I was not happy that I needed Leo's help to be honest. I wanted to be a modern, independent woman. But sometimes it's good to accept help, especially considering that my career was at stake.

★   ★   ★

'It is disgraceful,' said Greta Norris when I told her and Alf about what had happened over a tea of tinned ham and English salad. 'I've heard that it happens, but it is still awful for the women. Alf, why did you let such a thing happen?'

Alf looked at her sheepishly. 'He wasn't there,' I said, sticking up for him.

'That is not the point. You should take care of this girl, Alfred.' Greta spoke with a slight accent. 'I'm Austrian,' she told me over tea. 'It caused a lot of problems when Alf and I wanted to marry, after the war. When we met, I was an 'alien' and he was the local bobby sent to keep tabs on me. The superintendent he had then did not approve and tried to stop our marriage. I said to him, 'How can you disapprove? I am the daughter of a doctor and my family suffered more in the war than many others.' My mother was a Jew, you see, and she sent us out of Austria before the *Anschluss*. She could see what would happen.' Greta went quiet for a while.

'Do you like being a policeman's wife?' I asked her, after what seemed like a respectable amount of time. I had seen the films about the camps, and truly did not know what else to say in the face of such anguish. It made my own worries about how Kirkham and Porter treated me seem petty. Looking back, I wished I'd been better at saying the right thing. But Greta did not seem to notice or mind. Perhaps she was used to her family's experience rendering people speechless.

'I do now,' she said, breaking out of her reverie. 'Now we're in Stony End, in a house we rent privately, and I am more used to the shifts he works. When Alf and I first married we lived in a police house. The local inspector could call in at any time to check on the state of the house. Well, it was a nightmare, especially with young children, to keep everything tidy. But it all had to be spick and span at all hours of the day.'

I looked around Greta's neat little prefab. There certainly did not seem to be much out of place there, even without the inspector's spot-checks. Not like Annabel's cottage, which was littered with stockings and underwear drying on clothes horses, and piled high with the books we both loved to read.

'Then when the inspector had called,' Greta continued, 'word would get around, so the sergeant would call to see what the inspector had wanted. So you could not let your guard drop for a moment. Often the houses had no water or electricity. Some were not even fit to live in, yet we had to make them look perfect. If we spent money to decorate, often we'd be moved to a house and have to start all over again and some other policeman and his wife would get the benefit of the previous house. I also acted as an unofficial policewoman, doing many of the duties you do now, like helping to search or question females or typing up Alf's reports. But I was not paid for this.'

'Are you sorry you married me?' asked Alf.

'Of course not.' She smiled warmly at him. 'Well, not always.' She winked at me. 'Men — we do have to soothe their egos, do we not?'

'I don't have that problem with Leo,' I said proudly.

'Leo?'

'Bobbie is seeing Dr Stanhope,' Alf said. His voice became grim and I wondered why he also disapproved of me and Leo.

'Oh. Oh I see. Would you like some apple strudel, Bobbie?'

'I've never tried it,' I said, wondering what was not being said by Alf and Greta.

Five minutes later I was eating the most delicious pudding I had ever tasted. Greta also wrapped some up for me to take for Annabel. 'Thank you. She'll love it too, I'm sure.'

I thanked them for a lovely meal and made my way home, feeling warmed by their company and by the food. Greta was definitely a force to be reckoned with. Alf was certainly quieter in her presence, though it was clear that they loved each other very much. I pitied any inspector who suggested her house was anything other than spotless. But under her gruffness, she was also a kind woman. I imagined that she had no choice but to toughen up as an alien in a foreign country where she was distrusted.

I still had the strange feeling that things were being kept from me, and as a policewoman I should have been able to get to the truth. But it's only possible to find out the truth if people answer your questions honestly, and whilst no one had blatantly lied to me, I knew there was a lot being left unsaid. Plus, I was still finding my way in my new job. By the time I'd done six shifts of eight hours every week, learning so many new things as I went along, I was too tired to think of anything else.

I was to get answers sooner than I thought. Unfortunately those answers would lead to heartache.

7

When I got home from Alf and Greta Norris's, it was dark. Leo was waiting for me on the doorstep. I parked the Vespa and went to him.

'Sorry,' I said. 'I've had tea with the Norrises, and Annabel is on a late shift.'

'Don't worry. I just wanted to check you were okay after what happened today.'

'I'm fine, really. Do you want to come in for a cup of tea?'

It was the first time I'd invited him into the cottage, and the first time we had been completely alone. It's perhaps hard for today's generation to believe that we still had not kissed, but everything happened more slowly in those days. People seldom rushed into relationships, and my own experience with the Italian had made me cautious. I doubted that there were any dark secrets in Leo's life, but I still wanted to be sure.

He followed me through to the kitchen and stood with his arms folded as I made us a pot of tea. It felt as if he was protecting me from something and I liked that feeling very much. Yes I saw myself as a self-assured policewoman, but I must admit I also liked being a girl with a strapping handsome man taking care of me.

That night I remember feeling shy in his presence. Perhaps it was because we were completely alone for the first time. We sat in the lounge, drinking our tea, sitting next to each other on the sofa. Every time we inadvertently touched, such as when we both reached for the sugar, it felt as though electricity rushed through my veins. I laughed awkwardly.

'This is silly, isn't it?' I said. 'It's not as if we don't know each other well now.'

'I'd say we know each other very well.'

'Hmm,' I murmured. 'Though I still feel there's something you're keeping from me.' It was true. It was not only my work colleagues and the townspeople who seemed to be keeping a secret. I felt there was something about Leo too. "Tell me the truth. You've got a wife and eight children hidden up at Stanhope Manor, haven't you?'

'No, nothing like that.'

'So there is something.'

'It's nothing, Bobbie. At least nothing that should affect us.' He put his arm around my shoulder and I relaxed against him. His body was warm and strong and I felt I could trust him with anything. He put down his cup and then touched my chin, turning my face towards him. 'I would never do anything to hurt you.'

'I should hope not. I could have you locked up and the key thrown away.' I was joking, but it did not hit home. His eyes became dark. 'Not that I'd use my position to get revenge on a chap just because he didn't care for me,' I added hastily. 'I'm not that sort of girl, honestly, Leo.'

'I know you're not. You're lovely.' He stroked my cheek, his lips inches from mine.

Shyness gripped me again and I turned my head away slightly. I wanted that first kiss more than I could ever say, yet I was afraid of where it might lead. In reality I wanted more than just a kiss, but I knew I had to be careful. I had made one mistake by rushing into something. Unfortunately my body was not listening to my mind. Every nerve tingled and I felt a tight knot of anticipation in my tummy.

He turned my face back to him and his lips found mine, gently at first and then more passionately. In that moment I was his completely and all my resolve was lost. It did not matter about propriety. I wanted him and it was clear he wanted me. We started to slip down the sofa, as our lips locked. Leo's hands traced the outline of my hips . . .

Only the slamming of the front door

brought us to our senses. I jumped up off the sofa, almost as if my mother had walked in on us, rather than Annabel.

'Oh, I'm so sorry,' she said, grinning like a Cheshire cat. 'Why didn't you say you wanted the place to yourself?'

'I didn't. We didn't,' I stammered. 'Nothing happened.' Now I was treating her like my mother!

Leo stood up. He looked far more relaxed about the whole thing than I did. 'It's time I was going,' he said. He nodded his head briefly. 'Dr North. Bobbie.'

'I'll see you to the door,' I said, hoping for another of his wonderful kisses. But the mood had been broken, and we just said a quiet goodnight before he walked off into the darkness.

'So? When's the wedding?' Annabel asked, when I went back to the sitting room.

'Give us a chance. We've only just had our first kiss.'

'Oh, how sweet! You must tell me all about it over a glass of Babycham.'

The following morning, the sarge called me into his office. 'I hear there was an incident yesterday,' he said.

I weighed up the pros and cons of telling him. Whilst Porter was a little rat, it was not the done thing to tell on your colleagues, and he had been in the thrall of a man who was his senior. The inspector was also way above me and could make things very difficult not just for me, but for Sergeant Simmonds. As gruff as Simmonds could be at times, he was, I had decided, a decent man. There was also the issue that I did not want to appear like the helpless little woman who could not take care of herself, even if I had not quite managed to do so.

'Nothing I couldn't handle, Sarge,' I said, after all this ran through my mind.

'Are you sure, Blandford?'

'Yes, Sarge.'

'Because whilst some of the older members of the force like to adhere to their so-called traditions, I personally do not. Slavery used to be a tradition, but that did not make it right. Do you understand what I'm saying, Blandford?'

'Yes, Sarge. But . . . well if anything like that ever happened, and it came out publicly, it would look bad for the force. Wouldn't it?'

'Let me worry about that. It's not a concern any woman in my station should ever have.'

'I appreciate that, Sarge. Really I do. But . . . some things are best left alone.'

'Very well. If that's how you want to play it. I can guess your reasons. I think I may be one of those reasons, because I think you're a girl who worries about others too. But Kirkham has been trying to shut me down for a long time. It would just be another in a long line of battles I've fought against him.'

'Sarge, if you don't mind me saying . . . I think you just have to be careful who else you trust around here.' Porter and the inspector were clearly as thick as thieves.

'Don't think I'm not aware of that. Which is why, if you were to make a complaint, I could ensure that state of affairs did not go on for much longer.'

I was torn then. I should have told on Porter, and then the little squirt would have been out of the station for good. I still could not get past that taboo of telling on a fellow police officer. 'I can't, Sarge. I'm sorry.'

'I respect your decision, Blandford. More than you know. Now, you wanted a look at those cold cases, didn't you?'

'Yes, sir.' That brightened my day considerably.

'Good, that should keep you out of trouble and out of the way for a week or two. We keep all our archives in the cellar, and they're in a right mess. We just tend to chuck stuff down there when cases are closed and our filing system is nonexistent. So I'm looking to you to tidy the files up and put them into some semblance of order. If you've got time, I don't mind you reading over them. As long as the whole lot gets cleaned up.'

'I'd be delighted, Sarge. Thank you.'

The sarge gave me the key to the cellar and showed me the way. 'You lock the door every time you come out of there,' he warned. 'We don't want anyone being able to get in and tamper with evidence, even if it is in some old case from years ago.'

There was only one very dim light down in the cellar, and no heating. Even in summer it felt damp and cold. I soon came to realise that many of the file boxes were damaged, sometimes by the mould and sometimes by the bugs that lived off paper. Nevertheless, I was in my element down there.

I realised that before I could even start reading files, they needed to be sorted out. The main problem was that not only files had been dumped in the cellar. There were old typewriters, some from Victorian times, a couple of broken televisions, gas masks and other paraphernalia left over from the war, several telephones and switchboards, and all manner of office equipment that had been replaced upstairs with newer furnishings.

My first job was to clear a small corridor so I could get through it all. My next job was to create a place to work; so I emptied one corner near to the door and put an old desk, chair and typewriter in the space that was left. I stocked up with pens and reams of paper, thinking I could make a list of all the files and other equipment for easy reference. Just clearing the working space took me several hours, and I emerged from the cellar at break time, my uniform covered in dust and cobwebs, but with a strong sense of achievement. After a quick cup of tea and a Spam sandwich, I went back to continue my work.

There is something deeply satisfying about hard work. Despite the backache I suffered at the end of the day, I can honestly say that sorting out the cellar was my happiest few hours since joining the police force. I knew that once I had everything in its place, I could begin exploring the cold cases properly, so the back-breaking work was worth it.

It also kept me away from Porter just as the sarge intended. I had no wish to see or speak to him, and whilst I passed him as I went to the kitchenette, noticing that he kept his head down and avoided looking me in the eye, I did not have to deal with him.

I lost track of the time and the days as I continued my task. I woke up thinking of the cellar, and went to sleep thinking of it — when I wasn't thinking of Leo, that was; but even he took something of a back seat as I became absorbed with my task.

With the sarge's permission I donated some of the old equipment and office furniture to local schools and women's groups. I kept the bookcases and shelving for storage. Anything too damaged was taken to the tip. Eventually all that was left was me in my cluttered corner, empty shelves lining the walls, and the boxes of case files piled up in the centre of the floor.

It was over a week before I could sit down with the first box of files. None of them were in alphabetical order, so that was another job to be done. With the files to one side, and the typewriter to another, I began to make my list. It was difficult not to read each file, and I must admit to peeking more than once. I found out a lot about Stony End from those files. It had its fair share of larceny going back over the years, both petty and grand. Police cautions seemed to be the order of the day, rather than taking cases to court. I wondered whether this had more to do with the ties between the police and the community or because the officer in question just did not fancy having to go to court, with all the paperwork that entailed. I guessed it was a mixture of the two.

'You're supposed to be putting those

files away,' said the sarge one day, when he came down and caught me reading one.

'You said I could read them, Sarge.'

'At this rate, it will be a year before you finish this task and we need you on the beat. You can read them. Just make a list of those that interest you, and go back to them later.'

'Yes, Sarge.'

He grinned and left me to it. I don't think he expected me to really obey him. I tried to though. I really did. For the next hour I simply made a list of the files, then put them in their proper places on the shelves.

Then I found the file that changed everything.

I shouldn't have found it as quickly as I did. It was in a box in the middle of the pile, but when I tried to move the box on top of it, I found that they'd been stuck together by damp. I gave the top box a good tug and it tore open the lower box, spilling its contents out onto the floor.

'Damn!' I muttered. As I scooped the files up, one of them fell open. I found myself looking at the mug-shot picture of a teenage boy, taken by the police. He was holding a card with a number and there was something familiar about him. I knew his name before I even looked at it. It said 'Leo Stanhope', and gave his age as thirteen.

I picked up all the contents, my hands shaking in horror. I should have put it away. If his case was closed and his conviction spent, as many childhood convictions were, it meant that it did not matter anymore. Nevertheless I had to read it. I had to know why he had been arrested. I told myself he had probably just been scrumping apples, or maybe he smashed someone's window. Or knocked on doors and ran away. Just silly childish pranks that we all do.

But the list of charges inside the file said differently. It seemed that Leo had been something of a tearaway and had been given several cautions for stealing and for violent behaviour. Still, I told myself it did not matter. So what if he had been a wild boy? Lots of boys were. He had grown up to become a doctor. Surely that showed that he had been rehabilitated. Then I got to the last page, and the last charge against him.

'On the night of the 7th of September 1943, Leo Stanhope, age 14, was found on the Stockport Road in possession of a shotgun.' After that, the words became a blur on the page as my tears threatened to fall and obliterate them.

'The same shotgun was believed to have been used in the shooting of Police Constable Robert Blandford.'

8

'You knew I'd find it, didn't you, Sarge?' I said, walking into his office without knocking. 'Why couldn't you just tell me?' Mrs Higgins's advice to stay away from Leo suddenly made more sense. As did the odd looks some of the townspeople gave me and Leo when they saw us together.

Upset by what I had found, my mind drifted into paranoia, and I believed that everyone was in on it. I imagined them looking at me, pitying me for being such a sap where Leo was concerned. And him! Dear God, he had allowed me to develop feelings for him, knowing all along that he had killed my dad.

'It's a complicated story, Bobbie.' It was the first time the sarge had used my Christian name. 'Sit down, lass, and I'll tell you all about it.'

I ignored him, too angry to do otherwise. 'You knew he was my dad's killer, and you let me get close to him.'

'Shut the door and sit down, WPC Blandford.' His voice cracked the air.

That hit home. It reminded me that he was my superior. I did as I was told, closing the door and sitting down opposite him.

'You haven't seen the whole story,' the sarge said. 'You've only seen a snapshot of it. It's just part of the puzzle. And to be honest, there are still pieces missing. I wasn't here. I'd gone away to war.'

'Why isn't he in prison?'

'They don't send fourteen-year-olds to prison. They send them to reform school.'

I knew that, but all my legal knowledge seemed to have disappeared. All I could think was that my father's killer should have been in prison. Only my feelings for Leo stopped me from believing he should be hanged for the crime. Besides, I was never much of a fan of capital punishment.

'Besides . . . ' the sarge sighed heavily. 'Look, I have to tell this in the right order. Leo Stanhope was a good kid for most of his childhood. He came from a good family. The Stanhopes used to own the brewery, but Mapping managed to get it off them later. Don't ask me how. He — young Leo — did well at school, and passed his eleven plus. He attended the grammar school. Then when he was about twelve or thirteen something happened to him. I don't know what. I'd gone off to fight the war in Europe, and I heard a lot of this second-hand. Leo Stanhope started acting up. Most of it was trivial stuff to begin with. Trespassing, mild vandalism. Then he did some petty theft. And I mean petty. He stole bars of chocolate or bottles of beer from the off-licence. It's not like he needed to steal. His family gave him a generous allowance so he was never short of money. He did it for the kicks. Your dad tried to reason with him, and for a while it seemed like it worked. They got on well, and I'm told that Leo really liked your dad.

'Then one night, when your dad was on a job looking for some black marketers, he was shot. Several days later, Leo took his father's car. The police were alerted because he was underage and should not have been driving. When he was stopped, he had the sawn-off shotgun in the boot. They matched the bullets to the ones that killed your dad. So we thought we had our killer.'

'You thought?'

'Leo's elder sister, Julia, came forward and said that she was the one who shot your dad.'

'What?'

'She said she'd been involved with black marketers for some time, and that when your dad challenged her, she shot him.'

'Did you believe that?'

'The police at the time didn't know what to believe, but they had a confession, and she would not back down. She had been a troubled girl in her teens, much like her brother was in his, and some said she was a bit wanting in the brains department. She was once warned about her obsession with a married man. She'd made up stories about him, claiming they had a child together. It was all rubbish, of course. The fella threatened to take out a restraining order, forcing her to back down. She played the insanity card at the trial and various doctors, whom her parents had referred her to over the years, came forward and said that she was delusional, using her obsession with the married man as one of the symptoms. She was found guilty by reason of diminished responsibility, and sent to a sanatorium. She's been there ever since.'

'She covered for him,' I murmured. 'She took the blame for what Leo did.'

'That was the general consensus, yes. But . . . look, I'm not making excuses for him. Your father was my best friend. I'll never forgive myself for not being here that night. If I had . . . '

'You'd probably be dead too,' I whispered.

'That's possible. It's certain we'd have been out together. We always tried to get the same shifts. But what I'm saying is that from that moment, Leo Stanhope changed. He went back to his studies. The fact he's a doctor now proves that he's changed. He's become a pillar of the community, and that's why his record was expunged. Whatever mistake he made back then . . . '

'He killed my father!'

'I know, lass. I know. And nothing he or anyone else says or does is going to change that. I don't even know why I'm making excuses for him. For a long time I couldn't even look him in the eye. It offended me that he was still walking around when Robert was dead. Then I had reason to see him deal with someone who was dying — who would have died without his care — and I saw a different person. I began to wonder whether his sister really had been the one who killed your dad, because it didn't seem to me that Stanhope could take a life. Maybe it was one stupid mistake. Maybe the gun went off by accident. I don't know.'

'I have to find out the truth. Will you let me do that, Sarge?'

'You're too close to it, lass.'

'Please . . . I don't think you'd have let me near those files if you hadn't thought I would want to do something about it.'

He nodded as if conceding the truth of it. 'Okay, but you do it in your spare time. I'll let you look at all the records, but you must do the job we're paying you to do when you're on duty. What's more, the inspector must not know about it. He'd think it was a waste of resources, re-opening a case that was apparently solved nearly twenty years ago. The fact that it's your dad and a fellow copper will cut no ice with him.'

'I appreciate that, Sarge. Thank you.' I wondered if this was what the sarge had always intended. I also wondered if he had been mistaken in how quickly I would find the file.

'What is going to happen with you and Dr Stanhope?'

I shrugged. 'Nothing. Nothing is going to happen now.' That was much harder to accept than I thought. It's odd. You would think that finding out that a man you were falling in love with killed your father would be akin to hitting an iceberg, instantly freezing all feeling and emotion. Yet I remembered how kind and understanding Leo had been to me, and how lovely his kisses had been.

I shook off the feeling. I knew girls who had loved bad men. I had made a mistake myself with the Italian. A few moments of kindness and red-hot kisses did not make up for the bad in them. Leo Stanhope was a killer. What was more, he was a killer who had allowed his sister to take the blame for him. So maybe he was not as selfless as the sarge believed him to be. Perhaps, deep down, he still had that darkness that led him to being a wild boy. I had to arm myself against him, no matter how much it hurt. I would have to stop seeing him.

That turned out to be easier said than done. He was waiting at the cottage again when I returned home from work. Annabel had let him into the sitting room and then made herself scarce. He had that same wicked grin on his face, only now I saw it as something more sinister. The grin faded when he saw my grim expression. 'You know . . . ' he said quietly.

'Yes.'

'So where do we go from here?'

'Nowhere.'

'Bobbie, I'm sorry. I know I should have told you, but we were having such a good time, I didn't want to spoil it. I knew you'd find out the truth eventually. I suppose I was just postponing it. I don't know why Julia did what she did, but she's not me. I thought a lot of your dad. He tried to put me on the straight and narrow when I — '

'Oh listen to yourself,' I said, my emotions overtaking my common sense. 'You're still letting her take the blame for your mistake.'

'What?' He looked at me quizzically. 'You really think I did it?'

'Of course you did it. You had the shotgun in the car you stole. Go on, lie to me some more. Tell me it was a mistake. Tell me the gun went off by accident.' I realised I was repeating the sarge's words, and somewhere, deep down inside me, I wanted one of the excuses to be true.

'As you've obviously decided you're not going to believe me no matter what I say, I think the only thing I can do is leave.'

He stormed towards the door, almost knocking me over the back of the sofa as he did so. He caught my arms and put me upright. His touch burned me, and I was torn between shaking him off and falling into his arms. 'Sorry,' he said, his face stricken by an emotion I could not name. 'I'm sorry. I'd never

171

hurt you. Never.'

With those final words, he was gone . . .

*   *   *

'Oh, sweetheart,' said Annabel, when I'd told her the whole story. I sat curled up on the sofa. She had made me a cup of sweet tea, but it had not really helped. 'That's awful. But I really do believe he cares for you. He couldn't wait to see you today. He's changed lately. We've all noticed. He's friendlier with people, and everyone knows it's your influence.'

'What difference does it make? He killed my father, Annabel. How can we move past that?'

'Maybe he didn't. It could have been his sister. He's not responsible for what she does, though I know it's hard.'

'I have to find out the truth. The sarge says I can. Will you help me?'

'Ye-es . . . ' Annabel said slowly.

'What?'

'I'll help you, Bobbie, but I don't want you doing this for revenge. What I mean is . . . well, Dr Stanhope — Leo — is one of my superiors at the hospital. I can't start a witch hunt against him. I just can't.'

'Oh it doesn't matter,' I said, jumping up off the sofa. 'I'll do it myself.'

'Bobbie . . . '

I was not listening. I went to my room, overwhelmed by self-pity. I feel guilty now for the way I treated my best friend on that day. In fact, I feel guilty for a lot of things I said and did on that day and in the days that followed. Consumed by thoughts of revenge and an overwhelming need for justice for my father, I unearthed secrets that caused immense pain to myself and to others.

9

'Mrs Higgins? Are you in?' I knocked on the caravan door with one hand, whilst precariously perching a Victoria sponge in the other. 'I've brought you something.'

The old lady opened the door and smiled, but there was sadness behind it. 'I had a feeling you'd be along to see me, WPC Blandford.'

'This is an unofficial call,' I said, pointing to my civilian clothes. I was wearing blue jeans and a loose-fitting pink gingham shirt. My hair was tied in a ponytail. 'I'm not at work till later.'

'Come on in, dear girl, and I'll make us a cup of tea.'

Five minutes later we sat with our tea and generous slices of Victoria sponge, but silence had fallen. I did not know where to begin, and she appeared to be waiting for me to start the conversation.

I also had to be very careful what I said. Leo's record had been expunged, which meant that no one outside of law enforcement was allowed to know its contents. As angry and hurt as I was, I had been warned by the sarge that I could not pronounce him a murderer. At least not without Leo suing us.

'You knew Leo's — Dr Stanhope's — sister,' I said to Mrs Higgins at last. 'I mean, you knew why she was in the sanatorium.'

'Yes, I did. I used to be a . . . nurse there during the war. Head nurse.'

I was tempted to ask whether this was before or after Mrs Higgins had fought in *le Resistance*, but I held my tongue. I needed her on my side. Her pause before saying she had been a nurse in the sanatorium had not gone unnoticed, but I did not contradict her.

'You cared for her?'

'She was a sweet girl. A little on the wanting side mentally. Though in reality, she was not such a girl. She'd have been . . . let me see . . . yes, in her thirties at the time.'

'Did she ever tell you why she shot my father?'

'Oh dear girl, you're not talking about a person with rationality here. She would not be capable of the same sort of reasoning that you or I use.' Still in the interests of keeping on Mrs Higgins's good side, I let that one go. 'If I had asked for a reason — and it was not my job to — she would not have been able to give one. It would not have been a case that your father was in her way and had to be stopped. Or that she saw him as an enemy or danger to her. In fact, she might not even remember the moment.'

'That's interesting. About her not remembering. Is it possible . . . do you think . . . that she might have been covering up for someone else?'

'I see . . . I see . . . ' Mrs Higgins sat back against the caravan wall. 'You think . . . oh . . . well that would make a lot of sense. She was always talking about keeping her boy safe. She feared for him. Her demeanour towards her brother was always protective. He used to visit her every week. I think that's why he ended up becoming a doctor, because he used to talk to a lot of the doctors there about their work with the mentally challenged.'

'You warned me away from him,' I reminded her.

'Yes, I did. I've heard that you no longer see each other.'

Several weeks had passed since I had last spoken to Leo at the cottage. It did not really surprise me that everyone knew. They had all known that he was involved in my father's death, though whether anyone suspected him personally, I was not sure.

I had seen him in Stony End, and he had been in attendance at the police station once or twice when we had sick detainees to deal with. We had both behaved in a professional manner. Once or twice I caught him looking at me with that darkness in his eyes, and I daresay that once or twice he caught me looking at him too. I was wondering how I could be so wrong about someone. Yet seeing the kindness with which he treated even the most difficult prisoners made me wonder. Could someone make such a momentous mistake in their lives and then move on from it? Perhaps they could, but Leo's momentous mistake had involved my father. It was something that I could not move on from.

'Everyone knew about it but me,' I said, picking up cake crumbs with my fingertips and rolling them between my fingers. 'Yet no one said anything.'

'Well, you made such a lovely young couple. The past is in the past for a reason. What his sister did was dreadful and I realise it's hard for you to understand that. But when someone is in the grip of madness, they're not wicked or criminal. They . . . ' Mrs Higgins's voice tailed off. 'They can't help it.'

'Why were you really there?' I asked, feeling bolder.

'I told you. I was a nurse.'

I realised then how stupid it had been to think I'd get the truth out of Mrs Higgins.

'If you must know, dear, my husband had me committed,' she blurted out. 'Because I was not the docile little wife he wanted me to be. He convinced the doctors that I was delusional, because I was sure he was having an affair. It was all a ruse to get hold of my money and he eventually divorced me and married the woman he wasn't supposed to be having an affair with. It's such a wicked thing to do to someone — accusing them of being delusional. You start doubting yourself after a while. People, especially men, are too willing to believe women are mad. After all, hysteria is named after a woman's reproductive organs. Some men are afraid of women who show a lot of emotion.'

It suddenly struck me. 'Your husband . . . he wasn't the one that Julia Stanhope was delusional about, was he?'

'Oh no, dear. No. I've no idea who

that was. Apparently the man she was supposed to be obsessed with persuaded them not to name him in court as it was not considered relevant to the current case. He had friends in high places, obviously. Freemasons, I suppose. There are some very strange sects about.'

I sighed. How could I trust anything that Mrs Higgins told me? I smiled and thanked her for her time, leaving her with the remainder of the Victoria sponge.

My next stop was the courthouse in Derby, for the case transcripts. As they were a matter of public record, I did not need my official status to acquire them. They also knew me at the court, as I had often accompanied female prisoners or young offenders there, so they did things a bit more quickly for me. It took less than half an hour for them to track down the relevant files. Few others would have been allowed to take the files away, either. But I was a police officer, so it was okay for me.

I did not have time to read the files straight away, even though I was aching to. I was due on an evening shift, so I planned to leave them at the cottage for later. There would be parts of the case that were left out of the newspapers, and I hoped to find the name of Julia Stanhope's phantom male, reasoning that he might know something about the case.

I was coming out of the courthouse when I bumped into Inspector Kirkham. 'WPC Blandford,' he said curtly. He did not even have the grace to look embarrassed about his previous behaviour towards me.

'Sir,' I said, nodding my head. I was in my civvies, so did not bother to salute. I must admit that after what had happened, I found it hard to salute to him even if I was in uniform. I had no respect for the man. Of course I did salute when I had to, but it was always very grudgingly done.

'I heard you've been digging up the past.' He nodded towards the files I held in my hand. 'Some things are best left alone.'

'Is that an order, sir?'

He looked me squarely in the eye and I believe to this day that he really wanted to tell me to back off. 'It's not up to me what you do in your spare time with matters of public record, WPC Blandford.'

'No, sir.'

'But I will give you a warning, girl.'

I bristled at the way he spoke. Lots of Derbyshire men call women 'lass', and I did not mind that. But there was something malicious in the way he said 'girl'.

'What's that, sir?' I said, determined not to be bullied by him.

'If you want to do well in the police force, then it's time that you started to play the game. Other girls know when to make friends rather than enemies. It's time you learned. Don't cross me, girl. I can make or break your career.'

'Thank you for the warning, sir. Is it going to go on my record?'

'You know damn well it won't!' He made a sound that was something like 'gah'. 'Simmonds is too soft with the lot of you! Oh he pretends to be strict, but he's got a bleeding heart like the rest of them at Stony End. That's not the way to clean up the streets. One day such stations will be obsolete and it will all be run from the main headquarters. Then we'll see some proper policing.'

Looking back, I don't think Inspector Kirkham, who had spent too many years behind a desk, ever had an idea what 'proper policing' was. It was about being a presence on the street so that people, especially women, felt safe to go out at night or didn't have to worry if they'd forgotten to lock the back door. It was about frightened people having somewhere to go to if they noticed something untoward. Yes we dealt with a lot of time-wasters, but we sent them home feeling a little less scared. People trusted us in those days because we lived and worked amongst them. We knew their names and they knew ours.

The uniform we wore meant something. It could instil just the right amount of fear when needed, or it could inspire respect and comfort for someone who was having a bad day. The rise of Kirkham's style of centralised policing took all that away from the people, and from the police who cared to keep things as they were.

But it's fair to say on that day I did not know the future and did not think things could ever really change. All I knew was that a senior officer was threatening me, and I was very much concerned with my own problems as they stood. I needed a policeman whom I could trust and who would take away all the bad stuff for me, but I only had myself. All I could do was say good day to the inspector and walk on with my head held high. Meanwhile, my mind ran riot with all the scenarios in which he could destroy my career.

By the time I returned to the cottage, I had calmed down. If the inspector had wanted to end my career, he could have done it there and then by firing me. As a probationer I would have had little redress. So I told myself that he was just blowing hot air.

In a hurry, I popped the case files onto the coffee table, determined to read them when I returned. I trusted Annabel not to read anything of mine, just as I never read any of her patient files if she brought them home.

I was just coming out of the cottage when something struck me. There was no music from Mrs Garland's house. The song had been played several times a day for weeks and weeks and it invariably struck up whenever we were in the house.

Of course, Mrs Garland could be at work. Things at Mapping's had gone back to normal, with Mr Mapping's daughter and her male friend taking over the brewery. After a brief hiatus, the barrels were rolling out. They had changed Harris's dray for a truck. Gloria Mapping had swept her father's memory away in a very short time. The company were even rolling out a new beer called Mapping's Gold.

Call it copper's instinct or even women's intuition, but I felt a tingle on the back of my neck. There was something different about the silence coming from the house. Something final.

I went to the front door and knocked. As I did so, I felt sure I heard the back door slam shut. I went around to the back of the house and saw someone disappear over a wall. I thought I recognised him, sure it was Harris the dray driver, but before I could follow him my attention was taken by something else. There was a faint moaning sound coming from the house.

'Hello,' I said as I entered the house. 'Is anyone there?' I crept in wishing that, like my male colleagues, I could carry a truncheon. Listening for sounds of life, or of an attacker, I made my way through to the lounge.

Mrs Garland was lying on the sofa and I could tell straight away that she was not just sleeping.

10

I followed the procedure the police should always follow in such a circumstance. I had seen a dead body during my training when they took us to a mortuary, but that did not prepare me for what might be a murder.

My hands trembled as I knelt down next to the sofa and tried to ascertain if Jane Garland was still alive. I could see no blood, but there was an empty pill bottle on the floor next to a broken glass. Her mouth was open and I felt sure I heard a faint gurgling sound, but I was not sure. I put my fingers against Mrs Garland's neck and was able to feel a weak pulse. Putting my ear against her lips, I could feel her breath. I loosened her garments, guessing she had taken an overdose. I made sure her airway was clear before thinking about sending for help.

I hunted around for a telephone, only to find that the one in the house had been cut off, so I had to go out to the street. A young woman was passing by, pushing a pram.

'Excuse me,' I called. 'Please will you go to the box on the corner and telephone an ambulance and the police? Mrs Garland is . . . unwell.'

The girl turned out to be very quick to understand, and hurried to the corner whilst I went back into the cottage to secure the scene. As I did, I made notes in my notebook of everything I could see, meanwhile keeping a close watch on Mrs Garland.

It was only a few minutes before I heard the sirens. The sarge and Porter came rushing in, closely followed by the ambulance crew. Leo was with them, making the day seem even more unbearable. I had to remind myself that Jane Garland was having a much worse time of it than me.

'I think she's taken an overdose,' I

explained to him, trying to remain professional.

Leo was already on his knees checking on her. 'Mrs Garland,' he said, lifting her head slightly. 'Mrs Garland, can you hear me?' She made a guttural noise which was agonising to listen to. 'She's still alive at least, and I think you're right — she's taken something,' he said. He picked up the bottle.

'Erm . . . fingerprints,' I said ineffectually.

'I'm sure mine are on file somewhere,' he said darkly. 'It's more important I know what she's taken. They're antidepressants. I gave these to her last week, when she said she was not coping. I had no idea how bad she was.' He sounded disappointed with himself. He gave orders to the ambulance crew, telling them what to tell the doctors at the hospital. 'Show them this.' He handed over the medicine bottle, much to my chagrin. It was evidence! I wondered if there was a reason he did not want me to have the bottle, but he had already admitted to giving her the medication. Besides, why would Leo want her dead? I stopped the wave of paranoia. Of course the hospital would have to know what she had taken so they could help her. Evidence was the least important thing in such situations.

'Tell me what happened,' said the sarge after the ambulance crew had taken Jane Garland away. Leo hung around, saying that the doctors at the hospital would deal with her now.

'I heard someone rushing out of the back door, Sarge,' I said, looking at my notes. 'I was just about to pursue him.'

'You're sure it was a man?'

'I . . . er . . . yes, I think so. I mean, I know so. I think it was Harris, the dray driver. I was about to pursue him and then I heard Mrs Garland moaning. Anyway, I thought it best to let Harris go and instead I came in here and found her. I checked her pulse and she was still alive. I guessed it was an overdose.' I pointed to the broken glass.

'But that might be what he wants us to think.'

'Harris?'

'Yes, Sarge. Unless he found her this way and was startled.'

'Leaving her to die?'

'It doesn't look good either way,' I agreed.

'No, it doesn't,' said Leo. 'On the other hand, attempted suicide is a criminal offence, and sometimes we want to avoid that.'

'Are you suggesting we cover it up?'

'I'm only suggesting that until Mrs Garland is awake and able to tell us what really happened, we should keep an open mind,' said Leo. 'If someone tries to take their own life, WPC Blandford, there's usually a reason. The way they feel is punishment enough, don't you think?'

His use of my official name stung. 'I suppose so.'

'It's weak, if you ask me,' said Porter. 'A coward's way out.'

'Good job I didn't ask you then, isn't

it?' Leo glared at him.

The sarge interrupted. 'Blandford, come back to the station and give your report on Harris. We'll get some officers out on the street looking for him.'

'You don't think we should report the attempted suicide, Sarge?' I said.

'I think we'll be guided by Dr Stanhope at the moment. No need to cause the poor woman any more distress than necessary.'

It was my first experience of suicide, but I was to learn that the police and medical profession often did everything they could to avoid the prosecution of those who tried to take their own lives. In that they were often more understanding than the courts.

We left the cottage, with Peter Porter guarding the door. Leo got into his car without speaking to me and drove off. I got on my scooter and followed the sarge back to the station.

I gave my report about Harris, and other officers were sent out looking for him. But he had gone to ground somewhere, and his wife insisted she did not know where he was. Clearly he had recognised me too and knew he was in trouble. I thought back to that first day, when he had been coming from Mapping's and then lost everything off the dray.

'We've got Harris's boots,' said Alf Norris, coming back to the station after searching for him. 'We found them in the copse behind Mrs Higgins's place.'

'Are you sure they're his?' I asked.

'Oh yeah, they've got his name in. His wife says they're his spare pair.'

'I knew it was connected with that somehow,' I said. 'But why would he run through Mrs Higgins's yard, then come back? Have they found a weapon or anything? Something that was used to kill Mr Mapping? Maybe Harris dumped it there.'

'No, just the boots,' said Alf.

'Why would he take off his boots?' I tried to remember what Harris had been wearing on his feet that day, but my memory failed me.

I settled into my shift, wondering about Jane Garland and why she had taken such a drastic measure. Was it her love for Mr Mapping? I found out later that she had been sectioned and sent to a sanatorium. It was hard for me to admit Leo had been right, but it seemed sad to punish someone who was already going through so much.

That evening I was on foot patrol with Alf Norris. It was a fine night, so we strolled past the unity houses and out towards one of the small hamlets just beyond the estate. Called Little Stony, it was made up of rows of old stone cottages and farmhouses where elderly spinsters and retired army officers or schoolteachers lived.

'Why do you think Mrs Garland did it, Alf?'

'Well, there's been talk.'

'Has there? What about?'

'Her and Mr Mapping.'

'Yes, of course. I think she might have been in love with him. Annabel told me that she was very protective of him when his wife made allegations about his treatment of her. Tell me about it. For some reason, I haven't been allowed to know about the Mapping case. I don't even know what happened to the plaster casts I did of the footprints in Mrs Higgins's garden.'

'They're with all the other evidence, I think. We might be able to link them to Harris.'

'So who do you think killed him?'

'No one knows for sure. Mapping was not a popular man, except with women. He made a lot of enemies, but it didn't seem to bother him. He did Dr Stanhope's family out of the brewery. But that's not all. He was not kind to either of his wives. His daughter is just as ruthless as he is. A real chip off the old block.'

'What other evidence do we have? Annabel said something about a branding on his head.'

'Yes, it was done with one of the branding irons they use to mark the barrels. It's been suggested that he was held under the ale till he drowned.'

'Who are the suspects? His daughter?'

'She stood to gain the company, but she loved her father. They were a team and he would give her anything she wanted. Things changed a bit when her fella, Kenneth Truman, came along, but it would be more likely for Mapping to get Truman out of the way than the other way around. You see, Mapping has been suspected for a while of being involved in the underworld, and he knows people who know people. If you know what I mean.' Alf tapped his nose. 'But nothing we could ever prove. Mapping's got an older son, Bruce, but he's seldom around and doesn't want to take over the family business. He lives down in London with some arty types. He's not a man's man.'

'Oh.' I was not quite sure what Alf meant by that, but I did not want to press him. 'But they must suspect someone of killing Mapping.'

'I don't know, lass. Inspector Kirkham

has taken over the case. The sarge and Detective Sergeant Marshall are not happy about it, but it's out of their hands.'

'That's interesting,' I said. 'Inspector Kirkham tried to warn me off looking into my father's death today.'

'Did he now?'

'Yes. You don't suppose ... ' I stopped there. It was a huge accusation to make. I was always aware that I was getting paranoid. First Leo, now Inspector Kirkham. If I carried on, I'd be accusing all of Stony End of the murder of my father. 'Never mind.'

'That's probably the wisest thing you've said so far, lass,' said Alf kindly. ' 'Never mind' is safe. It means that you're not walking into the lion's den.'

'Don't you hate not knowing the ending of a story though, Alf? It's like somcone has ripped the pages out of a crime novel, leaving you not sure if the butler did it, or if it was the mad scientist from Russia . . . '

Before Alf could answer, an elderly

lady called us to her gate. 'I'm glad I've seen you, PC Norris,' she said. 'It's about time you did something about those drains.'

'The drains?' said Alf. 'They're not exactly my domain, Miss Cartwright.' I vaguely remembered Miss Cartwright telephoning the police station on my first day on the desk. I had suggested a plumber.

'I've tried to contact Mr Bernstein's people, but they say he's away and not due back for a while. They're not very happy with him, to be honest.'

'Mr Bernstein?' I asked.

'My neighbour. Went off to . . . oh, where was it? Berlin, that was it. Three months ago. He was due back, but now it seems he's gone off on some jaunt to the Holy Land. He's a Jewish gentleman, you see. But the drains have been smelling dreadful. I did ring the station, but whoever was on the desk just wasn't interested.'

I blushed, hoping Miss Cartwright would not recognise my voice.

'Come around the back,' she said, 'and you'll see for yourselves. Or smell for yourselves.'

We followed her to the back garden. It was not in our remit, but we were there to comfort people and set their minds at ease. As soon as we reached the back garden, both Alf and I knew. I immediately felt awful for not taking Mrs Cartwright's concerns seriously when she telephoned the police station. 'Go back inside, Miss Cartwright,' said Alf kindly. 'Put the kettle on and make yourself a nice cup of tea. We'll sort this out.'

It took a little more coaxing from Alf before Miss Cartwright went indoors, as she clearly wanted to know what was going on, but she finally left us. 'Go to the telephone box at the end of the road and call it in,' Alf said. 'I'm going inside.'

'I should come with you, Alf.'

'No, it's all right, lass. I don't think you want to see this.'

'Alf, I'm shocked at you, treating me

199

like this. I thought you were better than that.'

'Very well, if you insist on coming with me. But don't say I didn't warn you.'

Five minutes later when I was running out of the house, with a handkerchief pressed to my lips, I wished I had listened to him.

Mr Bernstein had not gone to Berlin or to the Holy Land. He had been dead inside his home for some time. There was no doubt about the cause of death. We found him lying on his bed with a knife wound in his chest.

Mail was piled up by the front door, and the electricity was off. One of the letters explained why. He had not paid the bill, so it had been disconnected.

Miss Cartwright, fortified by a cup of tea and a glass of sherry, told us this was not like him. 'He was a very meticulous man,' she said. 'Always paid his bills. I used to see him in the post office.'

'The electric's been cut off because

'Annabel,' I said, knocking softly on her bedroom door and opening it. 'Annabel, did you take my dad's case files?'

'Mmm? No, sweetie. Didn't know there were any. Where did you leave them?'

'On the coffee table. Did you move them?'

'No, there was nothing there when I came home. I do have to be up early in the morning, sweetie.'

'Sorry,' I whispered, shutting her bedroom door. I tried to remember where else I might have put them. I also tried to recall if I had locked the cottage door when I'd gone out earlier. I'd been distracted by the noise, or lack of it, from Mrs Garland's house. But no one in Stony End had to lock their doors. It was not that type of place.

I went back downstairs and hunted around the sitting room, to no avail. Slumping down on the sofa, I put my head in my hands. Someone had stolen the court notes, I was sure of it.

I wondered then what did they not want me to find out.

11

I parked my Vespa behind the station and went inside, fully expecting to spend a day on the desk. It was my turn on the rota. But when I entered reception, the sarge came out of his office.

'Come with me, WPC Blandford, I need you to help me question a woman.'

'Yes, Sarge,' I said, brightening up a little. I had spent a sleepless night worrying about the missing case notes, not least how I was going to explain it to the court.

'Porter, you're on the desk.'

'But Sarge . . . ' Porter had been skulking around trying to look busy. 'I'm on the beat today.'

'Not now you're not.'

'I have to be somewhere, Sarge.'

'Are you questioning my authority, Porter?'

'No, Sarge.' Porter's face reddened, but I could see by his eyes that he was livid with Sergeant Simmonds.

'Besides, if the inspector needs you, I'm sure he'll find a way to visit,' Simmonds said icily.

'I'm not sure what you mean, Sarge.'

'Really?' the sarge raised an eyebrow.

Porter looked down at his feet, and it seemed to me that he was hoping the ground would swallow him.

'Come on, Blandford,' said the sarge. 'We'll go in the Zephyr.'

'Do you think that Porter is snitching on us to the inspector, Sarge?' I asked as we drove out into the countryside.

'I don't think it, Blandford. I know it. Porter was sent here with some sob story about how he'd messed up at his last station, and that I was the only man who could put him right. But the inspector forgets that first and foremost I'm an investigator. I don't just take people at face value. Porter, whilst being a deceitful and sly little oik, has never messed up. He's too much of a bootlicker for that. That incident with you and the ink stamps convinced me of how close Porter and the inspector are. Then there was the thing with the moulds you took at Mrs Higgins's.'

'You mean the way he took credit for getting them?'

'Not that. The fact that he made sure the inspector knew about it. Have you seen or heard of those moulds since?'

'I thought they'd gone to Detective Sergeant Marshall. Alf said so.'

'Yes, but Marshall is hardly on top of things, even on a good day. They've . . . shall we say . . . been mislaid.'

'But why, Sarge?'

The sarge sighed, and I felt that he thought I was being obtuse. 'I'll not say much more,' he said in charitable tones. 'I want you to work this out for yourself. If you're as much Robert's daughter as I think you are, you'll get there in the end. But whatever you find out, I want you to come to me. Don't trust anyone else with it.'

I should have told the sarge then

she had never existed.

We were shown into the matron's office, and told to wait. Mrs Garland was being seen by the doctor and would be some time.

'I'm going outside for a cigarette,' the sarge said after five minutes. 'Come and get me when she's ready.'

'Yes, Sarge.'

A moment later a woman entered the office with a tray and two cups of tea. 'Oh, the sarge is outside,' I said, smiling at her. She was a very beautiful woman in her late forties or early fifties, dressed in a pale overall, and I assumed she was one of the auxiliary nurses. 'Is Mrs Garland ready yet?'

'I don't know,' said the woman, smiling shyly. 'I'm . . . I'm not a nurse.'

'Oh, I see.' I realised that she was a patient, and suddenly felt very afraid. What if she went crazy and attacked me? Common sense kicked in, and I told myself she was obviously a trustee. 'I'm WPC Blandford. And you are — ?'

At that her eyes widened, startled.

'Blandford . . . Blandford?' She looked at me with wonderment in her eyes. I saw her take in my hair and my face. 'Not Bobbie Blandford?'

'Yes, that's right.'

'You don't remember me?'

'No, I'm sorry. Should I?'

'I used to look after you when you were a little girl.'

'Did you? I don't remember. I'm sorry,' I said again.

'It's me. It's Julia Stanhope.'

It was my turn to freeze in horror. If what she had said was true, this was the woman who had killed my father. Or her brother had killed him and she had taken the blame. 'Julia . . . ' I whispered. 'Leo's sister?'

'You've seen Leo? How is he? Is he doing well? He tells me that he is, but he hasn't been to see me for a while and the last time he looked very unhappy. I must protect the boy.'

'He's doing okay,' I said cautiously, struck by her strange words. 'I haven't seen him for a while either.' I looked down at my fingers, which were knotted on my lap. 'But I'm sure he's all right. Why do you have to protect him? I realise he's your brother, but he's not a boy anymore. He's a grown-up and he can take care of himself.' I meant it in a comforting way, but she still looked worried.

'He's my boy,' she repeated, before leaving the room.

Her odd behaviour made me wonder how far she would go to protect him. Did it include taking the blame for his actions?

Before I had chance to think about what had just happened, the sarge returned.

'I've just met Julia Stanhope,' I told him.

'I see.'

'She's worried about Leo. She says he's unhappy. She also seems to think he's in danger.'

'In what way?'

'I don't know, but she kept on going on about how she had to protect her boy. I told her he's not a boy anymore. He's a grown man. But she's still fretting. I suppose that's the illness.'

'Yes, I suppose it is.'

The matron returned and told us that Mrs Garland was ready to see us. We were shown to a small bedroom in one of the far wings of the house. It was a pleasant if plain room, overlooking the park. Mrs Garland sat on the edge of the bed, brushing her hair. Where it had been in a bun most of the other times I'd seen her, it now fell in long tresses down her back. It softened her a little, but she also seemed sad.

She had the look of a woman for whom life had been a major disappointment. Her hair, which I guessed had once been chestnut brown, was streaked with grey, and her face was prematurely aged. Yet as with Julia Stanhope, there had once been beauty there. I then noticed that they were very much of a type — willowy and dark-haired, with fine cheekbones.

'Good morning, Mrs Garland,' said

the sarge. We sat down on two chairs that had been placed there for us. 'I would just like to ask you a few questions about what happened recently.'

'It was a mistake,' she said in a flat voice. 'I accidentally took too many tablets. What I mean is I took two then woke up and took two more, not realising how little time had passed. I did not mean to commit suicide.'

'Yes, I can see how that could happen. But actually that's not all I wish to talk to you about. What can you tell me about Mr Bernstein?'

I flashed a look of surprise in the sarge's direction. He had not briefed me and I had not expected things to go in that direction.

The sudden light in Mrs Garland's eyes was only momentary, but it was there, and suggested to me that she was more alert than she let on. 'He was a good friend of Mr Mapping. Mr Bernstein's family had owned a brewery in Germany. They liked to share stories

of different brews and brewing pro-
cesses.'

'Like Mapping's Gold, you mean?'

Mrs Garland looked down at the
floor. 'I don't know anything about
that.'

'Did Mr Mapping steal Mr Bernstein's idea?' asked the sarge.

'I don't know anything about that.'
She twisted her hands in her lap and bit
her lower lip so hard I thought it would
bleed.

'Tell me about your relationship with
Mr Mapping. How long did you work
for him?'

'I started working for him near to the
end of the war.'

'Was that before or after your son was
born?'

'What have you heard?' Mrs Garland
looked up, her eyes wide with alarm.

'What do you think I've heard, Mrs
Garland? Your son's name is Joseph,
isn't it?'

'That's right. He's at boarding
school. He's a very clever boy, my Joe.

Handsome too.'

'What did your husband do?'

'Joseph Senior was a pilot. He died in the war. His plane crashed over Belgium.'

'Yes, that's what I'd heard. But I've checked the military records and no pilot called Joseph Garland died in the circumstances you describe. Your father, on the other hand, is called Joseph.'

'I named my son after my father and my husband, what is wrong with that?'

'Last name too? Garland is your family name.'

'Very well,' she sighed. 'I had a child out of wedlock and when I came here I thought it best to be Mrs Garland. You know how people are.'

Jane Garland was not the only unmarried mother to ever lie about being widowed during the war. It was an easy lie to tell, because it was too delicate a subject to question.

'Your son was born in late 1946, at a home for unmarried mothers over near

Chesterfield. That was nearly a year after you came to work for Mr Mapping.'

'What are you suggesting?'

'Who is the father of your son, Mrs Garland?'

She heaved a big sigh. 'What's the point? They're already saying I'm delusional. You won't believe me.'

'We will,' I said, gently. 'Because Mr Mapping has a history of saying the women in his life are delusional, doesn't he?'

Jane Garland nodded sadly. 'I was so sure he'd be different with me,' she said dreamily, and I truly believed she was somewhere back in 1945, remembering all the empty promises she had received in the early days of their affair. 'I believed he was telling the truth when he said they'd lied. I forgave him even when he married another woman, insisting that it meant nothing and that it was only for political purposes. Then it came my turn and I found out he'd called me a liar too.'

'Is that why you killed him?' I asked. The sarge cast a sharp glance in my direction and I feared I'd overstepped the mark.

'I only did it for him . . . '

'Did what?' said the sarge. I think we both held our breath, waiting for the answer.

'Lionel told me that if I did what he wanted, he would finally claim Joseph as his and make him his heir. That he would marry me, despite what his daughter thought about me being too lower-class. She's a hard one, she is. But I honestly think she's the only woman he ever really loved. I didn't want to do it. Mr Bernstein was a nice old man. He always smelled of lemon drops, and when my Joe came home for a visit, Mr Bernstein would share them with him. There was a technique for making ale that Mr Bernstein had. It had made his family rich, before the Nazis took it all away from them. Lionel wanted the technique, but he did not want to pay Bernstein for it. He said it would cost him too much for the licence. Bernstein was greedy, Lionel said, but I really don't think he was.'

'What did Lionel ... Mr Mapping ... ask you to do?' I asked, understanding that we needed to get a proper confession.

'He did not actually say he wanted me to kill Bernstein. He only said that if Bernstein was dead, he'd be able to make lots of money. I said to him I'm not a killer ... ' She laughed harshly. 'I wasn't a killer,' she corrected herself. 'And Lionel said, 'No one is asking you to kill Bernstein. I'm just saying that life would be easier for us all if he was gone. We could get married and Joe would be legitimate. But don't ever say that I'm asking you to kill someone, Jane, because I'm not.' He was very clever about it really, knowing how much I wanted respectability.

'I went there late that evening, under the pretence that I had a message from Lionel. Bernstein was in bed, but he hadn't locked the back door. No one ever does around here. They never tell you in books how hard it is to kill someone. Or that if they're sleeping they wake up the first time you plunge a knife into them. I remember to this day the way his eyes accused me, but I think he was too shocked to speak . . . ' Her voice faded slightly. Then she became more matter-of-fact. 'You'll find the knife in the castle ruins. I went there afterwards. I was so sick . . . '

'What happened then?' asked the sarge. 'With Mapping? He broke his promise, didn't he?'

'No! It was the weekend so I wasn't back at work until the Monday. I never went up to Lionel's house. I telephoned him but the first thing he said was, 'Be very careful what you say on the telephone, Jane.' Then when I went in on Monday, early, I went to Lionel's office, but he was not there. I looked down over the walkway and saw him, floating in the ale.'

'You didn't push him in?' said the

sarge. He looked at me and we both frowned.

'No, why would I? We were going to be married.'

It seemed unlikely to me that having admitted one murder that Jane Garland would deny another, but she was not a stable woman. She might also have thought that one murder would get her into less trouble than two. At the time Britain still had capital punishment.

'I jumped up onto the dray whilst Harris wasn't looking, and then I got off near to old Mrs Higgins's caravan. I'd been wearing my own shoes, but I swapped them for Harris's old boots that he had in the back of the dray. I went through Mrs Higgins's garden then out through the copse. Then I changed back into my own shoes and walked along the road, as if I were going to work. I saw you there,' she said to me.

'He saw you,' I said, the light dawning. 'Harris saw you running through Mrs Higgins's garden. And he blackmailed you?'

She nodded. 'He needed the money for his new baby, he said. I told him to come back and I'd give him money when I had been to the bank. I did consider killing him, but after Mr Bernstein I really could not do it anymore. You have to believe me. So I thought, 'I'll teach him.' I took the overdose. I hoped that when he found me, he'd feel some sort of remorse.' She snorted inelegantly. 'He didn't even try to save me, did he? It was you, wasn't it?' She looked at me.

'Yes. I found you.'

'Thank you. I think . . . '

'Joe will be glad you're still alive,' I said, though it was of little comfort under the circumstances.

'Do you think so? I always feel I've been such a dreadful mother to him. I only see him in the holidays, and even then, I barely know him.' She shivered. 'I'm so afraid he'll grow up like his father and his half-sister. There is something missing with the Mappings.

Some spark of humanity.'

It seemed odd to hear that from a woman who had killed a helpless old man, and you may wonder at me feeling any sympathy for Jane Garland. Yet I did. It seemed to me that Lionel Mapping was like a poison that got under women's skin, driving them to insane acts. At that I began to wonder, but my thoughts at that time were not fully formed. I would be jumping ahead of myself in telling you the ideas I began to have as I listened to Jane Garland's story. Looking back from a distance it all seems so obvious, but it was not then because all the stories I had heard were fractured, like a jigsaw puzzle with half the pieces missing.

'So you're saying that you killed Mr Bernstein, but you did not kill Mr Mapping?' said the sarge.

'Yes, that's what I'm saying. I'm very sorry for what I did, but I loved him, you see. More than that, I wanted respectability for Joe. I wanted him to know his father. He was always asking about him. Will they let me see him, do you think? Joe, I mean. Will they let him come here?'

'I'll find out for you,' I said, when the sarge remained quiet. I know he was not happy with the outcome of the interview.

'Do you believe her, Sarge?' I asked as we drove back to Stony End.

'Do I believe she killed Mr Bernstein? Yes, and I think we'll find the evidence right where she said it was. Do I believe she *didn't* kill Mapping? I honestly don't know. It's a bit too convenient, him being dead, because he can't deny that he sent her to kill Bernstein. For all we know, Blandford, she could just be a mad woman who likes killing people. Or she might have thought Mapping wanted Bernstein dead when Mapping was really just thinking aloud, and took it upon herself to do it, to gain an advantage. We'll know when we get the psychiatric report, I suppose. But if she didn't kill Mapping, then who did?'

12

As Jane Garland had told us, the evidence of Bernstein's murder — a bloodied knife with her fingerprints on it — was found amongst the castle ruins. It was inconclusive, and she pleaded guilty in the magistrate's court before being sent to a higher court for sentencing.

'It's doubtful she'll go to prison,' the sarge told me on the morning she was due to be sentenced. 'The psychiatrist's report has come back and whilst they talk a lot of technical babble, it's clear she's lost her mind, though whether before or after the killing we don't know. I suppose that's for the court to decide.'

I had spent several weeks trying to piece together all the things I knew about both my father's death and

Mr Bernstein's and Mr Mapping's. I carried a scrap of paper around with me on which I had written down the salient points.

My father's death

Shot in line of duty whilst investigating a black market group during the war.

Dad befriended teenager Leo Stanhope, who was then suspected of shooting him.

Gun found in the car that Leo had taken from his father's garage.

Leo's sister, Julia Stanhope, took the blame for my father's murder but was sent to a mental hospital, deemed unfit to stand trial. She had apparently made up an affair with a married man and claimed to have had a baby, but was dismissed as delusional.

Then it struck me that I had missed something.

Where is the baby?

When would it have been born?

If Julia is delusional there would be no baby.

She is now at Acorn Lodge.

Reaching a blank there, I used the same piece of paper to scribble down notes about Mr Bernstein and Lionel Mapping's death. I put them together because they were connected.

Mr Bernstein and Mr Mapping

Jane Garland claims she murdered Bernstein because Lionel Mapping made strong hints that he wanted the old man dead. Because of Mapping's Gold?

As Mapping is dead there is nothing

to corroborate this. *So did Garland kill Bernstein for some reason of her own, then blame it on Mapping's influence?*

Garland also claims that she and Mapping had a long affair resulting in a child, Joe. But Mapping said (to whom?) that Jane Garland lied.

Jane Garland claims to have seen Mapping dead, but that she did not kill him. She left the brewery hidden in Harris's dray.

She was blackmailed by Harris (who has now been found and arrested but can add nothing more to the story).

<u>She is now at Acorn Lodge.</u>

'Has that scrap of paper told you anything yet?' asked the sarge, looking over my shoulder at lunchtime when I had gone to the kitchenette to make tea.

'I don't know,' I said. 'I mean . . . there are two women at Acorn Lodge. One who claims to have a child, but there is no child to prove it. And one who has a child who we know exists.' Joe Garland had apparently been to visit his mother a few days previously. He was staying with relatives in Yorkshire for a while. It seemed his time in boarding school was up. 'Who paid the fees for Joe Garland's school?' I asked.

'Now you're asking the right questions. It was through a trust. We're just trying to track down exactly where from. It's run by all sorts of holding companies. If rich men want to hide their doings, that's how they go about it.'

'Jane Garland would not have been able to afford the school fees on her income,' I mused, more to myself than to the sarge.

'That's right. Come with me, Blandford. We're going to ask some more questions about Mr Mapping.'

'She's not on his case,' said a voice

from the door. It was Peter Porter. 'You said she was to have nowt to do with it.'

'I've changed my mind,' said the sarge. 'Are you questioning my authority, lad?'

'But the inspector said — '

'The inspector is not here. Now why don't you go off and tell him tales, lad, whilst we get on with some proper policing?'

I left the kitchenette with my head held high that morning. I was taking part in 'proper policing' whilst Porter had been put roundly in his place!

'Where are we going, Sarge?' I asked when we got into the Zephyr. I wanted to be properly briefed this time.

'We're going to see Gloria Mapping. I've had word through from Poland about the technique used to make Mapping's Gold.'

I had not known Lionel Mapping and neither had I ever seen him, apart from one grainy picture in the newspaper which had told me very little. The portrait in his daughter's office was something quite different. It had pride of place behind her desk, and it showed Lionel Mapping as he had been in his youth, no more than twenty-eight years old. It also told me everything else I needed to know, including where Julia Stanhope's baby was. As I said, it was so obvious when that final piece of the puzzle fell into place. I still did not know everything, but I knew most of it then.

When we entered the office — I noticed that the sarge did not knock — Gloria Mapping and Kenneth Truman seemed to be having an argument and he was rubbing his jaw, which appeared to be bruised.

'Not now, Kenneth,' she was saying, pushing him away from her.

'Then when, Gloria? How long will you keep me waiting?'

'Ahem ... ' The sarge coughed delicately.

'Oh, Sergeant Simmonds,' said Miss Mapping, looking flustered. 'You really should have called ahead. We're rather busy. The inspector told me you would not be bothering us again.'

'I'm sure he did,' said the sarge. 'But he is not in charge of this investigation. I am.'

'I thought that was Detective Sergeant Marshall,' said Kenneth Truman.

'I've taken over. Just to clear up a few things.'

'Well I'm rather busy,' Miss Mapping said, sitting at her desk and shuffling papers.

'It won't take long.'

Without being asked, the sarge took a seat and gestured for me to sit down too. I had never seen him like this, but for the first time I realised what a good copper he was. Unlike the inspector, he would not be swayed by people who were richer than he, or who he thought had influence.

'Leave us, Kenneth,' Gloria Mapping snapped.

'But Gloria . . . '

'Leave us.'

Truman left the room, looking back

over his shoulder darkly.

'You know, of course,' the sarge began, 'that Mrs Garland is being sentenced today.'

'Of course. I'm glad she's off the streets. The woman has always been unstable.'

'Why do you say that?' I asked.

'Excuse me?'

'Why do you say she's always been unstable? As far as we know she worked quite well with your father for fifteen years or more.'

'Oh you can tell with a woman like that. They always keep it tightly locked up so that something has to give in the end. I mean, look at the rubbish she's spouting about her son being my father's. She's delusional. Probably got knocked up by some American soldier and thought she'd fool Daddy into thinking it was his.'

'Like Julia Stanhope,' I whispered. The sarge gave a barely detectable nod to let me know I was on the right track.

Gloria Mapping glared at me. 'What?'

'Julia Stanhope also claimed to have had a child by your father, didn't she? And she was also dismissed as delusional. Your father's second wife was dismissed as delusional when she kept going to the hospital with bruises and broken ribs.'

'My father never laid hands on that woman! In fact if anything he was weak around her. It was better when she died.'

'Why?' I asked, unsure exactly where the conversation was leading. But I began to have a feeling about Gloria Mapping. Call it a hunch, or female intuition. The clue, to me, was in the way she had shaken Kenneth Truman off and that bruise on his cheek. Neither was married, so there was no reason they could not have an affair. So I began to wonder what else was holding Gloria Mapping back. 'Because you had your father to yourself again?'

'How ridiculous. Is this what our taxes are going on, Sergeant Simmonds? Silly girls who think they can be detectives. It's unfortunate that my father liked women and they liked him. It was always getting him into trouble.'

'Miss Mapping,' I began, feeling that the sarge was letting me take the lead, 'was your father involved in the black market during the war?'

'Oh, I don't suppose it matters now,' she sighed. 'He had a little sideline going. Nothing serious. Nobody cares anymore, and people at the time were quite grateful.'

'But he tried to involve Leo Stanhope.'

'That idiot! Certainly not. Now his sister is another one who's delusional.'

'Yes, she claimed to have had an affair with your father, didn't she? One that led to the birth of a child.'

'How did you know that? I thought the court papers had been — '

'Stolen?' I finished for her, raising an eyebrow. 'It's true they were taken from my home before I could read them, so thank you for confirming that your father was the man Julia Stanhope named as the father of her child.' I hoped I was not blushing too much, and knew I would have to face the sarge with the truth when we were on our own again.

'You don't understand! He's dead now, so what would raking all that up have achieved? It was all lies anyway.'

The sarge spoke up. 'When did your father marry again?'

Miss Mapping seemed confused by the change in direction. 'It was about five years ago. I was away in America and came back and — '

'He had married someone else.'

'Yes. She was delusional too.'

'There's a lot of it about,' I said before I could stop myself. 'All these women your father knew; his second wife, Julia Stanhope, Jane Garland. All lying about his relationships with them. Did he lie to you about it? Is that why you think they're delusional?'

'He told me there was nothing in it.'

'Even his marriage?' said the sarge.

'She tricked him into it. Got to him

whilst he was lonely. It would never have happened if I had been at home.'

'Of course not,' I said. 'You must have been really angry when he said he intended to marry Jane Garland.'

'He would never have done it.'

'Well not now he's dead, no,' said the sarge.

'What are you suggesting?' Gloria Mapping had started to perspire.

'You were always very jealous of your father knowing other women, weren't you, Miss Mapping?' the sarge continued. 'After your mother died, you had your father to yourself for quite a long time. He had a relationship with Julia Stanhope, who I imagine is about the same age as you, but he backed off when she became pregnant and he told you that she had lied. Then he had to marry whilst you were away from home. And his affair with Jane Garland seemed to have lasted through all that time, producing a son whom he has been supporting for fourteen years. That son is now living with his mother's family in Sheffield. All the while your father insisted that Jane Garland was delusional.

'So to go back to my point, you must have been angry when he said he planned to marry her, after she had killed Bernstein. Or maybe he didn't tell you, because he dared not. Because he knew how you would react. The way you reacted when you hit his second wife, breaking her ribs. She covered up for you, because she was afraid and because she did not want to upset your father. Perhaps you overheard him and were so angry you finally decided to take your anger out on the person who really deserved it. The man who had manipulated all the women in his life, including you.'

'This is ludicrous. You have no proof of any of this.'

'No, that's true, we don't. However, we do have proof that the technique for making the ale called Mapping's Gold belonged to Mr Bernstein. The fact you're now producing that ale could make you an accessory to his murder.'

'It was Jane Garland. She killed Bernstein, then she killed my father because he didn't keep his promise to marry her.'

'But that still doesn't give you the rights to the technique, and I have it on good authority that some distant relatives of Mr Bernstein are planning to make a claim against your company. And so is Joseph Garland. Mrs Garland has said that she and your father did marry in secret, making Joseph a beneficiary to the estate.'

I looked sharply at the sarge. I had not heard about that. It seemed to be a shock to Gloria Mapping too, though she recovered her equilibrium very quickly.

'Let them do what they will.'

'Is that all you have to say?'

'Yes. Without evidence, you can't do anything.'

'Sadly she's right,' said the sarge as we drove away from Mapping's Brewery.

'Sarge?' I said.

'What?'

'Mr Bernstein doesn't have any relatives. They're all dead.'

'Yes, so they are. But Miss Mapping doesn't know that. Let her sweat a bit. She's got away with too much for too long.'

'You really think she killed her father?'

'Yes.'

'Sarge?'

'What now?'

'I don't remember Mrs Garland claiming that she and Mr Mapping were already married.'

'Don't you? Well, maybe you ought to pay a bit more attention then, Blandford.' He winked at me.

13

I fully intended to go and get some fish and chips then head home after my shift, so why the Vespa took me in the direction of Stanhope Manor I'll never know. It was not the first time the scooter had tricked me like that.

This time I took it right up to the courtyard near the front door, to save an embarrassing walk back down to the main gates.

It was only when I had my hand on the knocker that it occurred to me that Leo might not even be in. I knocked anyway, and almost did not wait for the door to open before fleeing back to the scooter. The door opened immediately.

'I saw you coming up the drive,' he said, standing with his hands folded.

'I needed to talk to you. About your father . . . '

'He's dead.'

'Yes, I know. He drowned in a vat of beer. Oh . . . ' I became flustered. I hadn't meant it to slip out like that. It was a good job I'd changed out of my uniform before leaving the police station.

'Lionel Mapping was not my father.'

'Oh but he was.' I ploughed on regardless. 'I've seen the picture in his office. I'm surprised no one else noticed. You're the image of him. And Julia is your mother, is she not?'

'Come in,' he commanded, looking around, as if afraid we might be overheard. It was unlikely. The manor house stood alone in the Peaks, and the nearest dwelling was a mile away. In all the time we had been seeing each other, I'd never been invited to the manor. We had always met in the pub or at the cinema, and he always dropped me back off at the cottage. Only now did I start to question why.

He led me through to the kitchen. It had all the signs of being the only room in the house that he used. There was a huge farmhouse table in the centre, and there was a high-backed leather arm-chair in the Chesterfield style next to an open hearth. The fire was not lit, as the weather was warm, but I imagined him sitting there in the evenings. Alone. The image made me feel sad, and yet I knew instinctively that it was the life he had chosen to live, and that even I had not breached it until this moment.

'Sit down,' he said, gesturing to an old-style wooden settle which was at the other side of the fireplace.

'Leo . . . I'm sorry. I didn't mean to blurt it out like that. I just thought you should know. If you didn't already. That's why she covered for you, wasn't it? Because you're her son.'

'I did not kill your father.'

'No . . . I know you didn't.' Truth be known, I still had not pieced everything together, but I did believe in his innocence. At the time I was well aware that I could have been as blinkered about Leo as Jane Garland had been about Lionel Mapping. Like father, like son. 'I know it's none of my business, and you've no reason to tell me anything after the awful things I said, but I would like to know the truth. Please.'

'I've believed, all this time, that my sister ... my mother ... really did shoot your father because Mapping had let her down.' He sat down in the Chesterfield and sighed. 'It's easier to start from the beginning, I think. For a long time, as far as I was aware, I was born to Harriet and John Stanhope. My sister, Julia, was eighteen when I was born, so I grew up thinking of her as my big sister and believed that I was a 'late' baby for my parents. Julia was very protective of me, but I had no idea at the time that it was anything other than sisterly love. She was a bit ... I hate to use the word simple, because in many ways she could be very clever ... but others have said she was wanting, and that's the only way to describe her. But there was no bad in her.

'My father — the man I called my father, John Stanhope — owned the brewery, amongst other business dealings. His family had owned the manor for hundreds of years, so he was by way of being the local laird too. Lionel Mapping's father had his eye on the brewery for years, and there was something of a feud between the families because of it. Julia always maintained that she and Lionel fell in love not long after Lionel's first wife died. He already had a daughter, Gloria, who was about eight years old when I was born, and Julia used to babysit her. Julia fell pregnant and I was passed off as the son of Harriet and John. That's what I believed, until I was twelve.'

'How did you find out the truth?'

'Julia told me. At first I didn't believe it, and thought it was one of her fantasies. She was getting worse every passing year. But when I looked at Mapping properly, I had to concede the truth. That's when I started to go off the rails a bit . . . a lot.' His mouth set in a grim line. 'I stole from shops, I damaged property. I got into fights with other boys. I'm not proud of myself. Harriet and John didn't know what to do with me. They were both rather ineffectual and more worried about what people would think than the fact that I was a kid crying out for help. I got that help, but not from my family.'

'From my dad,' I whispered, my eyes brimming with tears.

Leo nodded. 'Robert Blandford was the best man I ever knew. He could be really tough with me at times, and he pulled no punches in telling me I was headed for the hangman's noose if I didn't buck up my ideas, but it was what I needed. Julia was — I'm sorry to say — away with the fairies, and Harriet and John didn't have a clue. And because I listened to your father, he'd talk to me as if I were an adult. He understood what I was going through. I don't know if you know, but your father was — '

'Illegitimate,' I finished for him.

Leo sighed with relief. 'Then I'm not revealing anything you don't know.'

'Mum told me. She always said it was nothing to be ashamed of. Which, if you knew my mother, is really saying something, because she can be as stuck-up as they come. But she loved my dad, and accepted him for what he was. Sorry — you were telling me your story.'

'It ends about there. Your father helped me to see where I was heading. Then came that awful night when he was shot. I was so angry that the one person I could depend upon had been taken away from me. The following night I wouldn't have been in the car at all, but I received a call saying that Julia was in trouble over out near Stockport way and could I go to her. Harriet and John were out at some function, so there was only me.'

'Who called you?'

'I don't know. It was a girl and she said she was one of Julia's friends. I should have phoned the police, but when you're young and a bit stupid, you don't think of these things. I only knew that my sister — my mother — needed me, and there was no one left to tell me I shouldn't break the law, so off I went. I was pulled over on the Stockport road and they found the gun that killed your father in the boot.

'You know the rest. I was arrested, but Julia came forward and said that she'd shot your father to get Mapping, who was involved in the black market, into trouble because he denied their relationship. Harriet and John Stanhope didn't help. They were too afraid of the town knowing their daughter had had a child out of marriage, so they let Julia go to Acorn Lodge rather than admit the truth. And that's how Mapping got the brewery from them. He threatened to tell the world about me being his son.'

'But if he'd denied it that long, why admit it then?' It did not make sense to me and I believed that there was more to the story than Leo said. Either because he did not know or because he, too, was hiding something. But what else had he to hide? He had told me the truth about everything. If I were to believe he did not kill my father, then the phone call inciting him to drive to Stockport was interesting. There would be no way, after such a long time, of proving if that were true or not.

'He was probably banking on them being too embarrassed after living a lie for so long. They were weak . . . ' Leo spoke with something like distaste. 'If they had supported Julia when she had me, instead of trying to brush everything under the carpet, none of this might have happened.'

'Were you there when Mapping blackmailed your parents? Your grandparents . . . '

'No. Why, do you doubt my word?'

'No, really I don't, Leo. I believe everything you've told me. Only, everything I've heard about Mapping seems so . . . what's the word I'm looking for? Nebulous.'

'He was a very shady character.'

'So everyone says. I don't say that he didn't have a hand in the black market. Actually, one of mum's best friends was a black marketer. She was a lovely woman who saw us through the war with the things we couldn't get on ration. It was illegal, I know, but few people turned down black market goods when they could get them, so we're all guilty of complicity in some way. What I'm trying to say is that with Mapping, all he's supposed to have said to people is hearsay. Someone else heard it from their brother's best friend's cousin sort of thing. Either he was a very clever man who made sure no one could pin anything on him, or . . . ' I floundered there. 'There's something else you should know.'

'What's that?'

'You have a half-brother. Mrs Garland's son, Joseph. If she's to be believed.'

'So?'

'So . . . well he's been in boarding school and now he'll have to leave because there's no one to pay his fees now that Mapping is dead. Joe's mother's family in Sheffield are not very well off.'

'Are you're telling me that I'm responsible for him now? He's not my problem, Bobbie. He's Lionel Mapping's problem. Or he was.'

'But like you, his father has been denying him for years. And I can't imagine Gloria Mapping is going to help him.'

'Mapping paid his school fees regularly. That doesn't sound like denial to me.'

Leo had a point. Mapping had paid Joe Garland's school fees. It was one of the mysteries I could not solve and only added to my confusion about the sort of man that Mapping was.

'I just thought that as his mother has been taken to Acorn Lodge as yours was, because of her dealings with

Mapping, and Joe is not much older than you were at the time, then you might want to help him. Like my dad helped you.'

'Your father was an exceptional man, Bobbie. But I'm not him. And neither am I responsible for clearing up Lionel Mapping's mess.' His voice cracked out in the gloom of the kitchen.

'My father wasn't responsible for clearing up Lionel Mapping's mess, but he tried with you, and you weren't even a blood relative,' I snapped before I could help myself.

Leo stood up, his eyes as dark as the sky on a stormy day. 'If that's all, WPC Blandford, I have work to do.'

'I'm sorry,' I whispered. I stood up, my legs shaking. 'I'm sorry. That was unforgivable. I shouldn't have tried to make you feel responsible for Joe Garland. You're right, of course; he's not your problem.'

When he did not speak, I assumed that he agreed with me. I felt disappointed in him. I had wanted him to prove he was the hero I had believed him to be in the early days. But why should he care what I thought about him when I had mistrusted him and believed him capable of murder?

14

As I started back toward Stony End, my eyes filled with tears. I had made a monumental mess of things with Leo, and I did not know how to put it right. I had been so sure that he would want to care for Joe now that Mrs Garland would be locked up indefinitely.

I was wise enough to know that I was being unfair. Leo did not have to be my hero or anyone else's for that matter. He had the right not to become involved with Joe. As he said, the boy was someone else's mess. But I could only think that Joe was just a boy, and that with his mother incarcerated, his life would change beyond recognition. Then I thought of Leo and all that he had endured. It must have been a shock to find out his sister was really his mother. No wonder he went off the rails. But he had found his way back.

Who would be there to help Joe Garland?

I had to stop the scooter because I was crying so much. I was crying for myself as much as for Joe Garland. I had somehow managed to look at my father's death as a case from years ago, and that had given me some distance. Now, with everything that had happened, I began to feel what I had lost. Part of me even felt jealous of the time Leo had spent with my father. That should have been my time. Yet someone had denied me that, taking my dad away before I even got to know him.

Yet Leo had spent a lot of time with my dad, learning from him. If I had not been so stupid, he would have shared those memories with me. Now I had pushed him away and my father was further away from me than ever, as was the man I had fallen in love with.

I pulled into a siding about two hundred yards from Stanhope Manor and let the tears fall until there were no more. Some cars passed me, but no one stopped. I suddenly felt very alone. Annabel would be at work, my mother was miles away in Chesterfield, and I had no one else to whom I could turn in a time of crisis. What would I say, anyway? If I told them about Leo refusing to help Joe they might think badly of him, and I did not want that, even if I disagreed with him. I had lost him forever, because I was trying to make him responsible for Mapping's mistake. I wished I could turn back and tell him I was sorry again, but my last apology had fallen flat.

I barely heard the car pulling up next to me. When I turned around and saw it was Leo in his red sports car, my heart flipped.

'Leo . . . '

'There was a call for you from the station.' His voice was noncommittal, but his eyes were alert, and I wondered what he was thinking. 'Someone saw you coming this way earlier and guessed you were visiting the manor.

You're wanted urgently back at the station.'

'Oh, right, thank you. How did you know I was still here?'

'I was watching you from the house when the phone rang. Why are you crying?'

'It's been a long day,' I said, suddenly aware that my eyes were red and my nose was running. I sniffed loudly and pulled out a handkerchief. I would not be a pretty sight. 'I'd better get back.'

'No, you can't ride the scooter in that state. You'll crash. Leave it here and I'll take you to the station.'

'There's no need.'

'Doctor's orders.' He smiled a little. Honestly, I did not know where I stood with him! One moment he was furious, and the next he was acting like he cared what happened to me. It did not occur to me that he might be thinking exactly the same about me.

'You don't owe me anything,' I said, stiffly.

'Excuse me?'

'For whatever my father did for you. You don't owe me anything. You've repaid the debt by staying out of trouble and I know he'd be happy about that. You don't have to clean up *my* father's mess.'

He sighed and rolled his eyes. 'Oh for goodness sake, Bobbie, get into the car.'

I debated riding the scooter back to the station, but my nerves were shot to pieces, and Leo was probably right; I'd end up crashing. I locked the scooter up at the side of the road and got into Leo's car.

'I was thinking that you probably knew my father better than I did,' I eventually said after we had driven in silence for a while.

'I'm sorry.'

'No, really. It's not your fault. I like to think I remembered him, you see, but most of my memories were false and made up of anecdotes that my mother told me, like the time he tried to make an angel outfit out of crepe paper for a Sunday-school play and it fell apart when I walked up on stage, leaving me just in my vest and knickers. Until recently I had imagined it all happening at the Crooked Spire in Chesterfield. That could not be true, because now I know we lived in Stony End when my dad was alive, so it must have happened at St Jude's. Everything I thought I knew is being challenged, and now I don't know which memories of him are real and which I've made up in my head.'

'He was a good man, that's all you need to know.'

'But it's not fair,' I said heatedly. 'It's not fair that you and my brother Tom have memories of him and I don't. And I know it's not your fault, or Tom's, but it hurts so much . . . ' I took a deep breath, holding back the tears. 'But that's not your problem, so I'm sorry.' We were silent for a while longer.

'You ended up in just your vest and knickers in the church?' Leo asked.

I laughed a little. 'According to my mother I did. I was about three at the time and playing an angel in the nativity.'

'I may be able to help you with that.'

'How?'

'Leave it with me.'

When we reached the station the sarge was standing outside next to a vehicle I did not recognise. It was an old van left over from the war years. The sarge was also dressed in plain clothes of black trousers and a black roll-neck sweater. I'd never seen him out of uniform, but he still had that air of command, and it was rather attractive. 'Come on Blandford. I need your help. You're the only one I can trust with this.'

'Where are we going, Sarge? Do I need my uniform?'

'No, plain clothes are best. We're going to Sheffield on a stakeout.'

'Sheffield?' It was Leo who spoke. 'Is this something to do with what Bobbie was just discussing with me?'

The sarge glared at me. 'That all depends what she was discussing.'

'About Joe Garland,' I mumbled. 'I felt he had a right to know.'

'Oh you did, did you?' The sarge took a deep breath. 'Well maybe he did. I suggest you keep out of this, Dr Stanhope. It's police business. Come on, Blandford. We've wasted enough time already.'

'I'm coming with you,' said Leo.

'It's police business, sir,' said the sarge more formally.

'You may need a doctor.'

I looked from the sarge to Leo and back again. They seemed to have caught onto something that I'd missed, and I was a bit peeved at being left out of the loop. If I'd had more time to think about it, I would have worked it out. But things were happening so fast and I had so many things running around in my head, it was hard to get them all into a proper order.

The sarge nodded. 'Very well.'

'I'll follow you.'

'In that car? Are you mad?' the sarge scoffed. 'It's a bit conspicuous. Why do you think I've borrowed this old wreck?'

As the sarge spoke, Alf Norris came out of the station. 'It's been sorted, Sarge,' he said. 'You won't get any problems.'

'Thanks, Norris. Did you find out about that other thing?'

'Yes, Sarge. It's right where you said it would be.'

'Thank you. I'll deal with him when we get back. Come on, you two.'

'What was that all about?' I asked the sarge as we left Stony End.

'You'll find out when we get back.'

'That's all I need — more people being mysterious with me,' I muttered. 'I wish people would sometimes just say what they think and know.'

'Even though we're in plain clothes, I'm still your superior, Blandford.'

'Yes, Sarge. Sorry, Sarge.'

Leo and I sat huddled in the back of the van, which smelled vaguely of fish. The sarge drove like a madman over the Peaks, which meant we got thrown together more than once. 'Sorry,' I muttered when I fell into his arms. I noticed he did not apologise whenever he was thrown against me, and I don't know if it was wishful thinking, but I sometimes thought he held on a bit longer than was necessary.

'Are you all right now?' he asked me after we'd been on the road for over an hour.

'Yes, I'm fine, thank you.'

'I hated to see you so upset.'

'Like I said, it had been a long day. Things catch up with me sometimes. It was a bit unprofessional of me, actually.'

'What? To cry when you're out of uniform and think you're alone? Given the job you do, and what you're up against as a woman in the police force, I'm surprised you don't do it more often.'

'Stop it.'

'Stop what?'

'Stop being nice to me. I don't deserve it.'

Leo was just about to open his mouth to speak when the sarge pulled into a parking space. We were somewhere near the centre of the city, which had still not been properly rebuilt since the war. Amongst piles of rubble were terraced houses. Many had been pulled down and a development called Park Hill Flats was in progress, but it had not yet been finished. The sarge parked near to some rubble on a street where there were just a few houses standing.

It was dark and there were few street lamps. 'I hope we're not too late,' said the sarge.

I almost jumped out of my skin when someone knocked on the window next to the driver's seat. 'Sergeant Simmonds?' a disembodied voice said.

'That's me.'

'I'm Police Constable Reacher, South Yorkshire Constabulary. We've been watching the house since you telephoned us, but there has been no movement so far.'

'I know they're on their way,' the

sarge said. 'Keep a low profile but alert me if you see anything.'

'Very well, Sergeant. My sarge says we're to help you in any way we can.'

'Good man,' said the sarge.

'What do you think is going to happen?' I asked when the constable had gone back to his own lookout point. 'Is someone going to try to hurt Joe Garland?'

'That's what we suspect.'

'Because they think Jane Garland married Mr Mapping?'

'That's right,' said the sarge. 'Only I wasn't expecting things to happen so quickly. Luckily I'd told the South Yorkshire Constabulary to keep an eye out.'

'So tell us, Sarge. What do you think happened?'

'No, Blandford. You tell me.'

'I . . . ' I was a bit tongue-tied with Leo listening in. I felt I was being judged by both of them. But being there did help me to get a lot of my thoughts and suspicions into order. It at least verified the most compelling suspicion. 'I think Gloria Mapping is a very dangerous woman and has been for some time.'

'Go on,' said the sarge.

'I think that when her mother died, she could not bear to share her father with anyone, and that maybe he was a little bit afraid of her. That's why he denied the affair with Julia Stanhope and then again with Jane Garland. He only plucked up the courage to marry when Gloria was out of the country, but she made his wife's life hell, including being physically violent toward her. She — Gloria — may not have killed the second Mrs Mapping, but she probably contributed a lot to the poor woman's heart problems. Now, finding out that there's another possible heir to Lionel Mapping's fortune, she will do anything she can to stop him inheriting. That's what you were banking on when you let slip about the supposed secret marriage.' I paused for breath. 'But Sarge, that put

the boy in danger,' I said reproach-
fully.

'What else was I to do?' said the
sarge. 'We've no proof of anything. No
evidence against her. If we're going to
catch her, this is the only way. There's
more anyway.'

'What more?' I asked.

'Bobbie . . . ' Leo took my hand
gently. 'I think I know what Sergeant
Simmonds is getting at. When did you
realise, Sergeant?' he asked.

'Not till recently,' said the sarge.
'When it occurred to me how desperate
she might be to remove one obstacle.
And then when I realised how she's
been working things from behind the
scenes, like a puppeteer . . . well, it
stood to reason. I'm sorry if I ever
doubted you, Dr Stanhope.'

I was getting more and more
annoyed by their cryptic comments. 'If
someone wouldn't mind just saying
what you're talking about instead of
beating around the bush . . . '

PC Reacher knocked the window

again before anyone could tell me. 'Something's happening, Sarge,' he whispered.

'Come on,' the sarge said, getting out. 'Grab a torch from the back there.' I did as he said and clambered out of the back door of the van with Leo close behind me.

We crept amongst the rubble, trying to be quiet, but finding it hard with so much debris under our feet. We finally reached a mound behind which several other young policemen stood. It was dark, and the only light came from the street lamps and the torches the officers carried.

'It's number thirteen,' one of them muttered.

It was the end of a long row of terraces, next to an area that had been bombed during the war. By the streetlight we could still see the outline of the house that used to be attached to it. The line of the stairs, and the rooms above, and the remnants of wallpaper that had a nursery motif. I wondered where the baby who had slept in that room was. The worst of the blitz in Sheffield happened in 1940, so the child would be in their twenties by now. At least I hoped they were.

'One of the other coppers heard something around the back,' PC Reacher said.

'Right,' said the sarge in a low voice. 'Two of you go behind the house. Two of you stay here in case they try to escape through the rubble. Blandford, you come with me. Reacher, you're Sheffield Constabulary so I think you should lead us. Doctor, wait here with these men.'

'No,' said Leo. 'You may need me sooner than that.'

We were halfway across the street when we heard the sound of breaking glass. By the light of the moon, I could see the shadow of a car parked amongst another pile of rubble, far behind number thirteen. I prayed that number would not be unlucky for young Joe Garland.

We all ran for the front door. On the sarge's hushed orders (I did wonder then who was really in charge), PC Reacher did not wait for permission to enter. He kicked the door in and called, 'Police!'

The hallway was in darkness, but by the light of the torches we saw figures on the stairs. I waited for some noise from upstairs as the inhabitants woke up because of all the noise. Someone switched the downstairs hallway light on and the two figures were frozen in time, looking down at us.

'Stop right there, Miss Mapping,' said the sarge. 'And you, Mr Truman.'

Both turned around. Truman's face was stricken and he knew he was beat, but Gloria Mapping looked furious. She even tried to bluff it out. 'I came here to see my young brother,' she said.

'This time of night?' said the sarge. 'And by breaking the back window? Well, unfortunately he isn't here, so you've had a wasted journey.'

I should have trusted the sarge to

make sure the boy would not be harmed. He must have rung ahead to warn Joe Garland's relatives of the danger. It begged the question of why he had let Leo come along. Did he still not trust Leo? Or was there some other reason?

'Search them,' said the sarge, but before anyone could do anything, a shot rang out and I felt someone slumped beside me.

'Leo!' I screamed, catching him in my arms. 'Leo, darling . . . '

'I should have killed him years ago,' Gloria Mapping hissed as she was overcome by the sarge and Reacher. I sat on the floor with Leo cradled in my arms.

'Tell me what to do, Leo,' I said. 'Tell me how to help you.'

'I was too clever,' Gloria carried on, regardless of the horror before her. 'I should have shot Leo Stanhope instead of PC Blandford. He was my father!' she cried, and for a moment in the confusion of her garbled confession, I thought she was talking about my dad, before realising she meant Mapping. 'He was mine. Not yours. Not that other boy's. Not even Bruce's. He was mine.' Something in her had broken and her usual cool reserve had gone. It all came out then. 'But there was always someone trying to take him away from me. First that slut, Julia Stanhope, claiming to be pregnant. Then the Garland woman. Oh, Daddy thought I didn't know about him and her, but I did.

'And then my daddy decided he wanted to know his son. That fool there.' Gloria pointed at Leo. 'I had to do something. I thought I'd frame him for Blandford's murder, but Julia took the blame. It worked though. My father wanted nothing to do with either of them after that. He never knew it was me. Not till that last morning when he told me he was going to marry the Garland woman and accept the other boy as his own. Then Daddy learned what I was capable of. I told him how I'd beaten his wife and how I'd blackmailed the Stanhopes into giving up the brewery.'

She garbled on and on, but it was all much of a muchness once her initial revelations came out. 'I'm a genius,' she railed. 'I had it all under control.' Whatever control she had, had gone.

I only half-listened as I tended Leo's wound and waited for an ambulance. He had been hit in the stomach. 'Leo, tell me what to do,' I said. I knew that I had to keep my hand on the wound to stem the flow of blood. Not that I waited for him to tell me what to do. I was already doing it. I just wanted him to stay awake.

'Bobbie . . . ' Leo's eyes were glazed as he looked up at me.

'Yes, darling, I'm here,' I whispered, not caring that my colleagues could hear me.

'Bobbie, about Joe . . . '

'I'll take care of him,' I said, panic rising. 'Just until you're better.'

He closed his eyes and his face turned ashen grey.

15

'Some questions are never answered,' the sarge told me when we returned from Sheffield. We were in his office, going over the details. Debriefing, to use the modern parlance. I had been saying that I still did not understand Lionel Mapping's role in everything that had happened.

'I thought policing would be different,' I confessed. 'I thought there would be clues and red herrings and that the murderer would end up being obviously one person. But we have two murderers. If Gloria Mapping had not shot Leo . . . ' I paused a moment, the memory still too raw. ' . . . then we still might have had nothing on her. Apart from her breaking into Joe Garland's family's house.'

'A lot of policing is guesswork, hunches and damned luck,' said the sarge. 'You've seen the pile of unsolved cases we've got. Murderers seldom confess as easily as Jane Garland and Gloria Mapping did, and the evidence is never clear-cut. Especially in a public building that's used by so many people as Mapping's Ales is. Even old Mr Bernstein's house was not easy, due to the dust and debris from everyday living. Oh, you get the occasional crackpot coming and confessing. Some get a kick out of it. But the murderer is hardly ever the least likely person. It's nearly always someone the victim knows.'

'Did you know all along it was Gloria Mapping?'

The sarge looked as if he might nod, but he grinned. 'I'd love to say yes, Blandford, and take the credit. But no, I didn't. I had my money on Miss Garland all along. Their relationship wasn't exactly a secret to those of us who've lived in Stony End since the mid-40s. If I hadn't been warned so severely about bothering Miss Mapping

276

I might not have decided to investigate her. I did it in a fit of pique more than anything. Kirkham told me to lay off, and I hate it when he bosses me around.'

'I'm not sure I'm cut out for policing, Sarge,' I said, feeling sorry for myself.

'Why? Because you couldn't join all the dots? You had started to, Blandford. You just needed to trust your instincts a bit more.'

'I wanted to solve the case,' I admitted. 'I wanted to prove to you that I was worthy of the uniform. It's like . . . I hope you don't mind me saying this, but it's like you're my dad's brother and if I please you, I'll please him.'

'Sentimental nonsense,' the sarge said truculently, but I could see he was secretly pleased. 'None of us walk into this job knowing exactly what to do. But you did what you had to do. You went into that house in Sheffield with us without question, even though it was a dangerous situation. You're also good

277

with people. That's important for a copper.'

'I have a confession to make though, Sarge. I lost the court papers about Dad's case. I left them on the coffee table at home and when I went back, they were gone. That wasn't very professional of me. In my defence it was the day I found Jane Garland unconscious, but I know I should have been more careful.'

As I spoke the sarge opened the drawer in his desk and took out a familiar folder, dropping it on the desk in front of me.

'You took it?' I asked, puzzled.

'Why would I take it? I've seen it. No, it was someone else. Someone who is not going to be around here for much longer. Alf Norris found it in his locker.'

'Porter,' I said, the light dawning. 'We left him at Miss Garland's house.'

'Yep. Porter.'

'But I don't understand ... ' I stopped. Of course I understood. 'The inspector told him to take it.'

'Inspector Kirkham and Mapping were close friends. Apart from Bernstein, Kirkham was probably the only other male friend that Lionel Mapping had. They played golf together regularly. When Julia Stanhope's relationship with Mapping was brought up, Kirkham pulled some strings to have it left out of the newspaper reports. It's there though, in the original notes. Do you want to read them?'

I shook my head. 'It doesn't matter anymore. Not now I know it wasn't Julia or Leo Stanhope. I feel so sorry for both of them, living under this cloud for so long. I don't know if Julia really believed Leo had done it and protected him, or if she knew he had been framed and protected him. And he thought she had done it. It's an awful thing to be wrongly accused.' I could not deny my own guilt in accusing Leo.

We were still talking about the case when the door to the sarge's office opened with a loud crash. 'Sergeant Simmonds,' said Inspector Kirkham, 'what is the meaning of arresting Gloria

Mapping? She is the daughter of my oldest friend. And don't think I don't know that you had me invited by Greta Norris to keep me out of the way on the night you arrested her.'

The sarge stood up. 'She murdered her father and PC Robert Blandford, Inspector, and she intended to kill young Joe Garland. Dr Stanhope is also fighting for his life in a Sheffield hospital, after she shot him.'

'Who told you this?'

'No one had to tell us, Inspector,' I cut in, furious that the inspector was being so blinkered about it all. 'We were there on the scene when it happened.'

'Oh . . . ' The inspector looked abashed. 'Well, perhaps she feared for her life. Stanhope was a dangerous character in his youth.'

'We have a confession, in writing, from her very lips.'

'Under duress, no doubt.'

'There is one thing I don't understand,' said the sarge, ignoring Kirkham's insult.

'What's that?' asked the inspector.

'How she managed to get young Joe Garland's address so quickly. I had thought it would take her a few days to track him down, yet only a few hours after I told her he was in Sheffield with relatives, she knew where to find him.'

'I have no idea why you're asking me,' said the inspector, 'but I'd be very careful about making accusations if I were you, Simmonds.'

'It'll come out in court anyway,' said the sarge. 'Let's just hope that whoever gave her the address has friends who can keep his name out of the court papers.'

It was like watching two prize fighters, albeit with one way past his prime. The sarge was definitely winning on points.

'They might have been misled into thinking she intended to help the lad.'

'Yes, let's hope that's the reason.'

'Very well,' said the inspector. 'We'll say no more about it.' He turned to leave.

'There is one last thing, sir,' said the sarge. 'I'd like Porter reassigned.'

The inspector turned back. 'Why?'

'I don't trust him.'

'He stays here.'

'In that case, I'll probably have to ask him what possessed him to steal sensitive court documents from WPC Blandford's home. He's a weak lad, and should be easily bullied into spilling the beans. Much better that he leaves without a fuss, don't you think, Inspector? We don't want a scandal.'

And that's a knockout, I thought to myself, on seeing the inspector turn a funny shade of green.

★ ★ ★

Summer had given way to autumn, then to winter, and somehow over a year passed since I first arrived in Stony End. Before I knew it, it was 1961. John F. Kennedy had become the first truly handsome American president, causing us all to fall in love with him, and

Annabel and I had become hooked on a new television series called *Coronation Street*, which had started in December 1960. We were particularly caught up in the passionate love life of Elsie Tanner.

It was almost time for the policemen's ball again. Most of my time had been taken up with the trial of Gloria Mapping (when I was not selling tickets to the ball). Unlike Jane Garland and Julia Stanhope, the courts were not convinced that Miss Mapping was mad, which was ironic considering she turned out to be the most unstable of the three women involved in Lionel Mapping's life. Her coldness, which she re-acquired after her rabid confession, did not endear her to the jury. They saw it as a lack of remorse and they may well have been right. She was found guilty of murder, attempted murder and conspiracy to commit murder and sent to prison to await execution.

Those of you who know the history of capital punishment in Britain will know that she did not go to the hangman's noose. Ruth Ellis was the last tragic woman to be hanged. Miss Mapping's sentence was commuted to life imprisonment. It is difficult to say how I personally feel about that. On the one hand I am opposed to capital punishment, but on the other hand this was the woman who killed my father and in doing so, cast a shadow over the lives of two innocent people, Leo and Julia Stanhope. Years later, Gloria Mapping really did go mad and was sent to a high-security mental hospital, where she died in the 1970s.

Her accomplice, Kenneth Truman, received a lighter sentence, and as far as I am aware, died destitute in the 1980s, never having returned to Stony End. He maintained that Gloria had promised to marry him if he did as she asked, and he was so much in love, he went along with it. It was his evidence against her that settled her fate.

They both turn up sometimes in those books or television shows on famous murders. I've even been quoted or appeared in some of them. Of particular interest to a salacious press is Miss Mapping's adoration for her father. Some hint that there was more to their relationship than she let on, otherwise she would not have acted like a jealous lover whenever he had an affair, but I don't know about that. There was nothing sexual about her love for her father. It was more blind adoration, and the longing of a little girl to be the only one in her father's life.

Her brother, Bruce, came back to Stony End briefly, to sell up the brewery. Most of the money went on his sister's defence.

Lionel Mapping himself continues to be a mystery to me and to those who discussed the case for many years afterwards. Was he a weak but charming man in fear of an obsessed daughter, who had to keep his love affairs secret? Or did he manipulate the women in his life just as his daughter manipulated her lover? He had played his cards close to his chest, trusting few people, except

Inspector Kirkham, and Kirkham never responded to requests for information. In fact, in the years that followed, the inspector would tell everyone who asked that he had never really liked the Mapping family and was only ever on nodding acquaintance with them.

I was on the beat in Stony End on a bright sunny morning when a familiar red sports car pulled up alongside me.

'Leo . . . You're home!' Remembering my professional status, and feeling suddenly awkward in his presence, I stammered, 'It's good to see you well, Dr Stanhope.' There was a teenage boy sitting in the passenger seat. Dressed in the beatnik style of the day, with dark hair flopping over his eyes, he showed every sign of growing into a handsome young man.

'You look really well yourself, WPC Blandford. This is my brother, Joe.'

'I'm glad to meet you at last, Joe,' I said, swallowing back a lump in my throat. Seeing them together like that touched me in a way I had not expected. 'When did you get back to Britain?'

After the court case, during which time I only saw him sporadically, Leo had gone abroad to convalesce, leaving me heartbroken, even though I had no right to expect anything from him. Especially after believing he had killed my father. He had come home briefly to pack but at the time I had gone to visit my mother in Chesterfield. The reopening of my father's trial had affected her badly, and I suspected that in some ways she was angry with me. The upshot was that I had missed Leo by just a few days when I returned.

'Yesterday,' said Leo. 'Joe is due back at boarding school next week, so I'm just getting him settled into the house. We've had a good time in America, haven't we, Joe?'

Joe nodded. 'Yeah, it was cool. Leo said we can go back there again sometime.'

'That's lovely,' I said, feeling a bit jealous. Package holidays were only just taking off (excuse the pun), and I had personally never been further than Blackpool. I also ached to think that Leo had not rushed back to be with me.

'We were settling Julia in,' Leo said, as if explaining himself.

'Julia?' I remembered hearing that she had left Acorn Lodge not long after the Gloria Mapping case.

'Yes, she's living over there for a while. They have some wonderful psychiatrists, and she's staying in a place near to the sea. One day she might be able to come home, but for now, she feels she can't cope with Stony End.'

'I'm sorry,' I said, feeling selfish for thinking of my own feelings. 'I, erm . . . I'm selling tickets for the policemen's ball. It's Friday night. Would you like some?'

'Are you going to be there?'

'I don't know.' I didn't have a date, and hated the idea of going alone, but I did not want to tell him that. He might think I was hinting.

'If you go, I'll go. Otherwise I'll have no friends there. I'll drop Joe off at the pictures. Right, Joe?'

'Yeah . . . I want to see *Spartacus*.'

'All right then,' I said, smiling broadly. We may never get back to how we were before, but at least he saw me as a friend now. I sold him his ticket and we parted ways.

I was walking along the main street when a young woman accidentally bumped into me. She was wearing a neat blue suit and a pill-box hat, and was remarkably pretty. 'I'm sorry, miss,' I said. 'Verity? It is you, isn't it?'

She looked horrified, and glanced around to see if anyone heard me. 'Yes, it's me. Please don't say anything. I've got a good job at the bank now and I don't want my employers to know I was on the streets. I'm old enough,' she added for good measure.

Doing a quick calculation, I realised that she must be over sixteen at least, and judging by the way she was dressed, she was doing well for herself.

'It'll be our secret,' I said. 'I'm so glad to see you. I've worried about you many a night. Have you got time for a cup of tea? I'd really like to know how you're doing.'

'Yes, I'm on my lunch break.'

'I managed to sort myself out,' Verity explained over a cuppa in the café. 'With the help of a social worker, I went back to school and did my O-levels and everything. I remembered how kind you and the other constable were when I came to Stony End. I'm sorry I ran away now but I thought you'd try to send me back home. Anyway, when I saw a job going in the local bank I thought I'd come back. I'm lodging with Miss Cartwright over in Little Stony. You won't tell though, will you? I mean about my previous life. Not Miss Cartwright.'

'No, of course not. I'll make sure PC Norris doesn't either. I'm so proud of you, Verity. Just promise me that if you're ever in trouble again, you'll come to me for help.'

'Guide's honour,' she said with a smile. 'I have to go or I'll be late for work.'

I left the café with a smile on my face. Leo had returned and was talking to me, and Verity had also done well for herself. I couldn't take any credit for that. I certainly had not been the heroine I imagined myself to be when I first found her in the public loos and vowed to straighten her life out, but it did not matter. It was more important that Verity herself had done it.

Okay, I admit I felt a bit victorious, so on the way home I called in to see Mrs Higgins to see if she would come to the policemen's ball. It was my attempt to ease her back into the world. I can still hear her laughter now as I walked away from the caravan having admitted defeat.

On Friday evening I put my best dress on. I had been taking style tips from Annabel, and wore a gorgeous full-skirted white lace dress with matching gloves.

'You look like Grace Kelly,' Annabel said when I did a twirl in the living room. She was dressed in black satin.

'No, you look like Grace Kelly. I'm too ginger.'

'Do you know how many women would kill for your hair, WPC Blandford?'

'Really? I was always teased about it at school. Where's your date, by the way?' Annabel had been seeing another junior doctor at the hospital.

'Oh he's been called out on an emergency.'

It was probably uncharitable of me, but when Leo did not turn up at the policemen's ball, I hoped it was because he had been called out on the same emergency. I did my best not to miss him, dancing with other young policemen who had come over from the headquarters to make up the numbers. But I suspected they were only asking me because Annabel was otherwise engaged with a detective who was visiting from London.

'He's married,' I hissed at her when we went into the loos. 'You can tell by the way his shirt is ironed. Single men never iron that well.'

'Oh I know that, Sherlock,' she said. 'But we're only dancing, and he's buying the drinks.'

'Oh well, that's all right then,' I said archly.

'You're only sore because Leo hasn't turned up. He probably is out on that emergency, you know.'

'Perhaps. Or perhaps he hasn't really forgiven me.'

The music played, ten or more years out of date, was a bit old-fashioned for my taste. It was the sort of music my mother liked, like Nat King Cole and Mario Lanza. The rock 'n' roll revolution had not quite reached the British police force. So the dances were rather staid waltzes or two-steps. This was a pity, as Annabel and I had been practising our jitterbugging for weeks.

The night was to get worse. PC Porter had arrived with the inspector, chasing behind him like a little lap dog. He grinned at me maliciously and took to the dance floor with a young woman who clearly did not know his reputation. When he had finished with her, he came to me and asked, 'D'ya wanna dance?'

'No, thank you.'

'Yes, come along,' said the inspector, who was nearby. 'Don't let the side down, Blandford. Let's have our young people making friends.'

It seemed I had no choice but to dance with Porter. I stood as far away from him as the dance would allow, as 'Goodnight Irene' played. I've hated that song ever since, forever associating it with Porter's clammy hands on my waist and his leering eyes trying to get a peek at my cleavage.

Then he was violently dragged from my arms. I was surprised, but not exactly upset about it, though it was perplexing to see him lying on the ground all of a sudden. At first I thought — hoped — it was Leo, passionately jealous to see me dancing with a man we both saw as an enemy, but I looked up to see a man I had never met before. He was huge, over six feet tall, and nearly as wide. He picked Porter up by the scruff of the neck.

'Do you know who I am?' the man asked.

'No,' said Porter. 'Put me down. There's a penalty for assaulting a police officer.'

'Good, then I hope they arrest you for assaulting my missus. Has nightmares about it, she does.'

'Your missus?' Porter's eyes were wide with terror.

'Deidre Bennett as was. Now Mrs Deidre Fletcher. She finally told me what you did to her. Stamping her like she was vermin.' I racked my brains and then remembered that Deidre Bennett was the WPC who had lasted only a week before I'd joined the Stony End station.

'It's tradition,' said Porter. 'Just a bit of fun.' At which point, Mr Fletcher pulled back his fist and socked Porter clean in the jaw, knocking him to the ground again.

The odd thing was that none of the policemen present stepped forward to help Porter. Normally they looked after their own. Their lack of response told Porter clearly that he was not one of their own. Even the inspector was silent, though I suspected that he was afraid of being implicated and earning a sock in the jaw himself.

Porter stood up, trembling. 'I am placing you under . . . '

'Let's not get hasty,' said Sergeant Simmonds, stepping forward. 'Everyone's had a bit too much to drink and we're here to raise money for a good cause. No need to make any arrests. It would only mean a full investigation into the events, and then it would all come out in court.'

'Yes, let's do that,' said Mr Fletcher.

'Sir . . . ' Porter looked towards the inspector.

'I, erm . . . Well, in this instance we'll

let it go,' said the inspector, but I did not like the hateful look he gave the sarge as he left the ballroom, with Porter following behind looking a bit less like the happy puppy he had been on arrival. He would have a swollen jaw by morning and whilst I abhor violence, I have to say it could not have happened to a nicer man.

'Sarge,' I started to say, concerned more about what the inspector could do, but Simmonds had already gone to talk to Mr Fletcher. Judging by his gestures, he was apologising profusely. Fletcher, who obviously recognised and respected a stronger personality, began to calm down and the rest of the party went back to what they were doing.

I was in a glum mood when I went back to the seats at the side of the ballroom. Especially when they started playing 'Save the Last Dance for Me'. Not one of the young policemen had saved it for me, and Annabel went straight into the open arms of the detective.

I was about to leave and go home to lick my wounds, when Leo came rushing in. 'I'm so sorry,' he said, taking me straight into his arms and onto the dance floor. 'Mrs Harris went into labour three months early. She lost the baby.'

'Hasn't Mr Harris been in prison for the past seven months?'

'I didn't ask . . . ' He pulled me close and it was as if we had never been apart. 'Anyway, that's not our problem.'

'I thought you still hadn't forgiven me.'

'For what?'

'For thinking you killed my father.'

'You believed what Gloria Mapping wanted everyone to believe.'

'But I should have believed in you. I'm so sorry, Leo.'

'Then you're forgiven.'

'And I shamed you into taking Joe on.'

'Yes you did.'

'Oh.'

'But that doesn't mean it was the

wrong thing for me to do. He's a lot like I was at that age.'

'He seemed nice enough. I mean . . . ' I blushed. 'He doesn't look like a tearaway.

'He has his moments. But I don't want to talk about that now. It's that song again. 'Save the Last Dance for Me'. Shall we make it our song?'

'Can we not?'

He looked taken aback. 'Okay, if you'd rather not.'

'It's too tied up with Jane Garland and the way she was about Mapping. If we're going to have a song, which would be wonderful, I'd much rather we found our own. But first let's start again, with no secrets and no recriminations. Please, Leo.'

'I'd like that,' he said, showing his wonderful smile. I had missed it so much. He kissed me passionately. I had missed that too. 'Yes,' he said, holding me so close I could barely breathe. Not that I minded. Being breathless in Leo's arms was a pleasure. 'Even if it takes us a lifetime, one day we will find our own song.'

★ ★ ★

The music stopped and our evening was over before it had even begun. Or so I thought.

'Will you come up to the manor, Bobbie? I've got something to show you.'

'Hmm, I've heard that before. What is it?' I laughed. 'Your etchings?'

Leo smiled. 'Something far more precious than that. I'll make sure that you return home with your honour intact. Trust me?'

I nodded. Yes, I did trust him. He had his car waiting outside, and drove us up to the manor house. When I got out of the car, it struck me that the house looked different, even in the dark. With welcoming lights shining in some of the windows, it looked like a home.

'Come on,' Leo said, gently, taking my hand as we got out of the car. 'This is a special surprise for you. I'm only sorry it's taken me so long to sort it out.'

'You've been ill,' I said. 'And you've had your brother and Julia to sort out. So you're forgiven for whatever it is.'

He led me into the house and then along a corridor to what appeared to be a ballroom. A large white sheet filled one wall. 'Is it ready, Joe?' he asked in the darkness. It had not occurred to me that his brother would be there, and I felt a little bit disappointed that we would not be alone. Still, I was the one who told him he had to care for his brother, so I could not really complain that the boy was now going to be a part of our lives.

'Ready,' said Joe. I could just make out his shadow at the back of the ballroom. The middle of the sheet lit up into a white square.

'Is it a film?' I asked. '*Ben Hur*, perhaps?'

'Better than that,' said Leo. 'Sit down.' He held out a chair for me and he sat in the one next to it, both of us facing the makeshift screen. 'When you told me about the day you ended up in your drawers and vest on stage in the nativity I vaguely remembered it. My adoptive father, John Stanhope, was an amateur film-maker and he enjoyed filming local events. So Joe and I have been searching through all the film. Roll the camera, Joe.'

The screen flickered into life and black and white images moved before our eyes. There was no sound, only the silent formation of children as they arrived on stage one by one to begin the nativity. In the foreground it was possible to see the heads of the audience watching. At the end of the queue of children, a tiny moppet with a shock of hair clambered clumsily onto the stage. 'It's me . . . ' I whispered. 'It's me, isn't it?'

'I reckon so,' said Leo.

'But it might not be.'

'Just wait.'

The next thing that happened was

me — three-year-old me — tripping over my dress and the whole thing falling apart, leaving me in my underwear. I burst out laughing just as the little me burst into tears. 'Oh no! It's every bit as awful as Mum said. I'll never be Elizabeth Taylor. I wish I hadn't seen this now and I'm glad I forgot!' But I was laughing as I said it.

'Wait,' Leo whispered again. 'There's a better memory coming for you.'

Someone in the foreground stood up and rushed to the stage. It was a man, and he took off his uniform jacket then picked me up in his arms. When he turned around to face the audience, I saw that it was my handsome dad. I had only ever seen photographs of him, but the cine-camera brought him to life in a way two-dimensional photos never could. In that moment he was alive for me again. He held me to him, wrapping his jacket around me, soothing me as I cried at the ignominy of it all. Although I could not hear him telling me not to worry, I knew he was saying it. He put his helmet on my little head. It was the message I had been waiting for. I knew then that he approved of me joining the police force.

The screen froze there, with him holding me in his arms smiling and me, swamped by his uniform, smiling back at him through baby tears.

My hero. My dad.

THE END

We do hope that you have enjoyed reading this large print book.

Did you know that all of our titles are available for purchase?

We publish a wide range of high quality large print books including:
Romances, Mysteries, Classics
General Fiction
Non Fiction and Westerns

Special interest titles available in large print are:
The Little Oxford Dictionary
Music Book, Song Book
Hymn Book, Service Book

Also available from us courtesy of Oxford University Press:
Young Readers' Dictionary
(large print edition)
Young Readers' Thesaurus
(large print edition)

For further information or a free brochure, please contact us at:
Ulverscroft Large Print Books Ltd.,
The Green, Bradgate Road, Anstey,
Leicester, LE7 7FU, England.
Tel: (00 44) 0116 236 4325
Fax: (00 44) 0116 234 0205

HOLIDAY ROMANCE

Patricia Keyson

Dee, a travel rep, flies to the south of Spain to work at the Paradiso hotel. On the journey, a chance encounter with the half-Spanish model Freddie leads to the two spending time together, and she suspects she may be falling for him. Then Dee is introduced to Freddie's uncle, Miguel, who is particularly charming towards her — despite having only recently been in a relationship with fellow rep Karen. But when Karen disappears in suspicious circumstances, Dee must decide which man she can trust . . .